THE HUMAN MEANING OF HIROSHIMA—THEN AND NOW

For Kaz Tanaka, the atomic age began with a fluttering scrap of white, like a tiny piece of paper, coming out of a high-flying B-29 bomber.

For Larry Johnson, it began with a shaft of incredibly bright light in the Nevada desert.

For Ted Van Kirk, it began with a beautifully executed job of navigation.

For five-year-old Dorothy Burns, it began with the joy of knowing her Daddy was coming home.

This fascinating, thought-provoking book takes us inside the initial event, into the minds, into the memories, into the feelings of those who lived it—and are still living it.

THE END OF THE WORLD THAT WAS

Six Lives in the Atomic Age

PETER GOLDMAN has been hailed by the *Wall Street Journal* as "perhaps the best writer in American journalism." He is Senior Editor at *Newsweek* magazine, and his previous books include *Report from Black America*, *The Death and Life of Malcom X*, *Quest for the Presidency 1984* (co-author), and *Charlie Company: What Vietnam Did to Us* (co-author).
Peter Goldman lives in New York City.

By Peter Goldman and Tony Fuller (with others)

Charlie Company: What Vietnam Did to Us
The Quest for the Presidency 1984

By Peter Goldman

Civil Rights: The Challenge of the Fourteenth Amendment
Report from Black America
The Death and Life of Malcolm X

THE END OF THE WORLD THAT WAS

Six Lives in the Atomic Age

by Peter Goldman

*with Pamela Abramson •
Lucille Beachy • Tracy Dahlby •
Martin Kasindorf • John McCormick •
Wally McNamee*

A Newsweek Book

A PLUME BOOK

NEW AMERICAN LIBRARY

NEW YORK AND SCARBOROUGH, ONTARIO

NAL BOOKS ARE AVAILABLE AT QUANTITY DISCOUNTS WHEN USED TO PROMOTE PRODUCTS OR SERVICES. FOR INFORMATION PLEASE WRITE TO PREMIUM MARKETING DIVISION, NEW AMERICAN LIBRARY, 1633 BROADWAY, NEW YORK, NEW YORK 10019.

A hardcover edition of *The End of the World That Was* has been published simultaneously by E. P. Dutton, a division of New American Library, 2 Park Avenue, New York, New York 10019, and, in Canada, by Fitzhenry & Whiteside Limited, Toronto.

PLUME TRADEMARK REG. U.S. PAT. OFF. AND FOREIGN COUNTRIES
REG. TRADEMARK—MARCA REGISTRADA
HECHO EN HARRISONBURG, VA., U.S.A.

Library of Congress Cataloging-in-Publication Data
Goldman, Peter Louis, 1933–
The end of the world that was : six lives in the atomic age.

(A Newsweek book)
1. Atomic bomb—History. 2. Atomic bomb—Social aspects. I. Title.
QC773.G58 1986 940.54'26 85-23308
ISBN 0-525-24428-X
ISBN 0-452-25806-5 (pbk)

Designed by Fritz A. Metsch

First Plume Printing, May, 1986

1 2 3 4 5 6 7 8 9

PRINTED IN THE UNITED STATES OF AMERICA

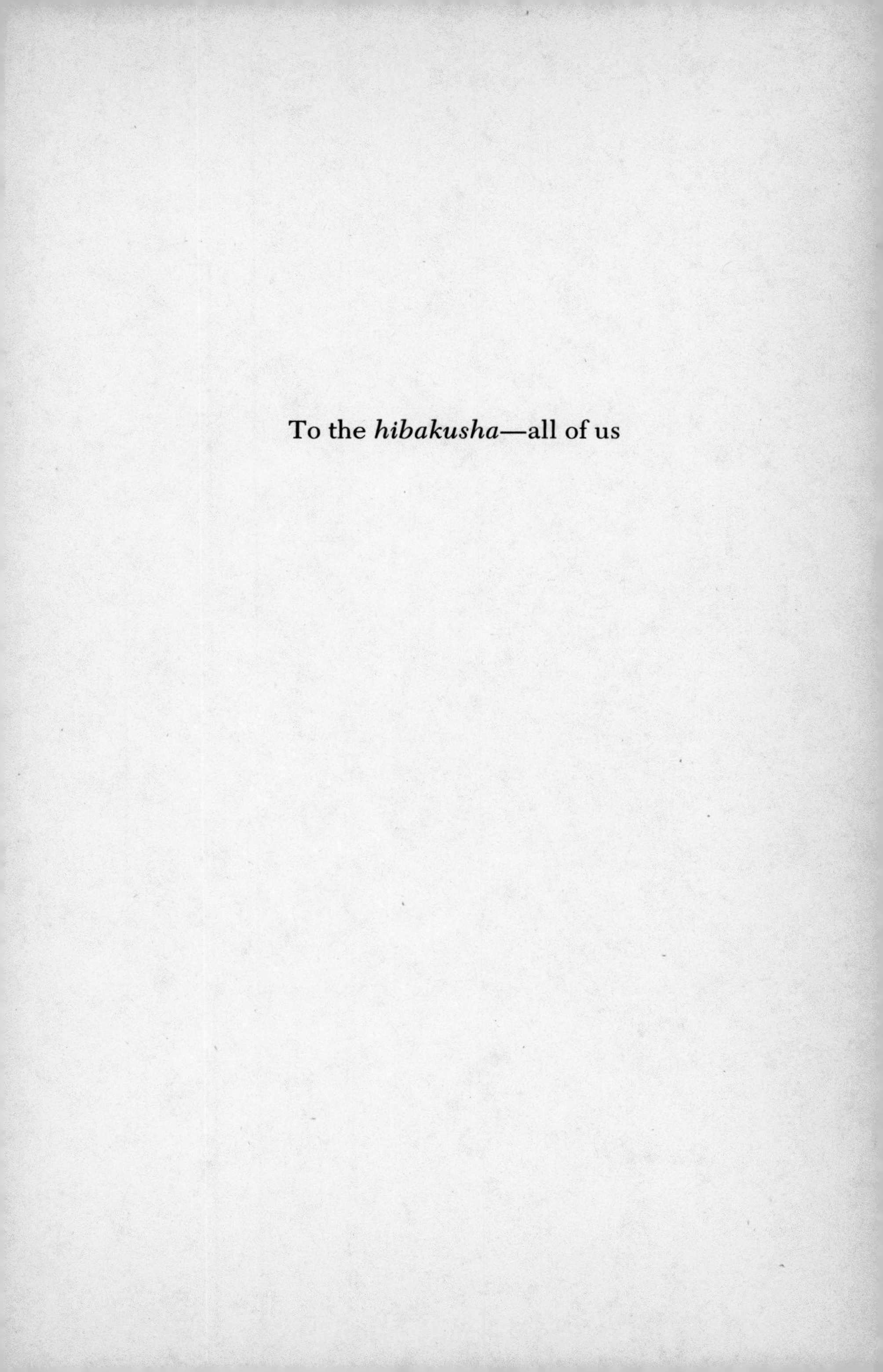

To the *hibakusha*—all of us

Preface

IN THE SUMMER of 1945, the human race, by its own choice and its own invention, became an endangered species. The instrument of its peril was called the atomic bomb and was the creation of men—scientists, soldiers, and politicians—who had only inexact knowledge of its destructive power and of its implications for the survival of mankind. A crude prototype was tested in the New Mexico desert on July 16; its secret ingredients included Scotch tape and Kleenex, along with a core of fissionable plutonium, but it was powerful enough to shake the earth, turn the night to noon, and raise a mushroom cloud seven miles high. In a flash of cosmic light, the world had entered on the atomic age and has lived at risk ever since, hostage to the bomb and to ourselves.

The stopped clocks of Hiroshima placed the beginning of that age a bit after 8:15 in the morning of August 6—the moment at which the first operational bomb exploded over the heart of what had been a bustling seaport and turned it into a city of the dead. Seen from a distance, the nuclear dawn had a certain biblical beauty, like a vision out of Genesis; an eight-year-old schoolgirl named Kay Okubo stood in awe beside a stream in the countryside and watched the mushroom shape rise up from behind a mountain, forty miles away. The view at first hand was a glimpse of the inferno, a city become a mass funeral pyre. A young man named Kanji Kuramoto joined in the weeks thereafter in the work of cremating the victims, burning as many as twenty bodies himself in a day. He had hoped to find some trace of his father among them, but did not. His only inheritance in the ashes was the stench of death; it would be thirty years before he could wash the memory of the smell from his hands.

The story in the pages that follow is the collective memoir of a number of men and women caught up in the events of the nuclear summer of 1945. Among the six principals in the narrative, one was a scientist who helped build the bomb. One was the armaments officer who loaded it aboard the bomber *Enola Gay;* his daughter, forty years later, was working for its abolition. One was the navigator who steered it to Japan. Two were among its targets and saw it fall; they became members of a new caste called *hibakusha,* or bomb-affected persons, one still living in Hiroshima, the other in the United States. They were strangers whose lives intersected for a millisecond at a point called Zero, 1,980 feet above central Hiroshima, and were altered by what happened there, as the world was altered.

They were players in and witnesses to the larger drama, not its prime movers; the decisions to build and drop the bomb were taken by other, grander personages. Those decisions were debated then and have been questioned ever since, from that comfortable vantage point called historical revisionism. What the inquest has sometimes neglected was the *inevitability* of the bomb —the tides of discovery and war commanding its invention and, once invented, its use. "The book of nature is there for all to read," Isidor I. Rabi, the physicist and Nobel laureate, mused long afterward; if he and his associates at Los Alamos had not found the secret, someone someday would have.

Neither was it likely that America, having the means to end the bloodiest war in human history, would not employ it. Some of the scientists who made it argued against its use on human targets; one of them, Edward Teller, proposed exploding a demonstration bomb thirty thousand feet over Tokyo, a light show intended to scare the enemy into submission without actually hurting anyone. The idea was rejected, for reasons that seemed sound in their day to the generals managing the war and the fliers assigned to the mission. Until the test in the desert, it was by no means certain that the bomb would work, and even afterward, there remained the possibility of a misfire. "Suppose you lined up the world, built bleachers and gave out five thousand tickets," Paul Tibbets, the pilot of the *Enola Gay,* mused forty years on, "and it turned out to be a dud?"

The possibility that the bomb might not be needed at all was likewise weighed and discarded. One such recommendation, little remarked in histories of the bomb, came from a subpanel of the United States Strategic Bombing Survey (Us-Bus for short), a civilian commission set up in 1944 to study the effects of the air war against Germany and its utility against Japan. The bomb was still in gestation when Vice-Chairman Paul Nitze, a Wall Street banker in the early stages of a long and distinguished public career, and a group of Us-Bus colleagues were asked in the spring of 1945 to undertake a special assignment: proposing a single basic strategy to bring Tokyo to its knees. Doing it with nuclear weapons alone was one of six options then on the table, but the bomb had not yet been tested and was still viewed with some skepticism in Washington; the man from War Mobilization who brought Us-Bus the assignment made plain his own suspicion that it wouldn't work.

Nitze and his colleagues concluded that it wouldn't

matter—that America could win without dropping the bomb, *or* invading Japan, *or* coaxing the Russians into the war. What they proposed instead was a combination of conventional bombing and a picket line of submarines; the objective would be what Nitze described years later as "the piecemealing of Japan," isolating its component islands so completely from the world and from one another that they could no longer sustain a coherent war effort.

Nitze himself came to believe in retrospect that they had been perhaps too sanguine—that they might have underestimated the ferocity of the Japanese in defense of their home islands. Still, the recommendation was taken seriously enough to be sent forward to President Truman, and from him to the Joint Chiefs of Staff for comment. They rejected it on the principal ground that an invasion *would* be necessary. Their judgment was colored by their experience in the European theater; a total war could not be definitively ended, in their view, until the enemy's capital had been occupied and his leader captured or killed. Plans for an invasion were accordingly in train when the bomb became available, a swifter, surer, and far less costly way to end the war. The men who ordered its use believed it would save as many as a million American lives.

Yet the questions first raised in 1945 have continued to torment and divide us. Rabi for one was grateful for the bomb and its success; still, when Japan surrendered a week after Hiroshima, he could not bring himself to open the bottle of Johnny Walker Black he had laid away for a victory toast. As the shadow of the bomb has lengthened since, the doubts and second-guesses have proliferated. "Nobody at Los Alamos would have dreamed of ten thousand atomic weapons," another of its galaxy of Nobelists, Hans Bethe, surmised in retrospect. But the world had fifty thousand by the middle 1980s, some with as much as a thousand times the power of the Hiroshima bomb, and Bethe found his own seven-year-old grandson tortured by waking nightmares of nuclear war.

Such nightmares had become part of the common lot of mankind. In a Louis Harris poll in 1983, two-thirds of all Americans expected a nuclear war sometime in the next twenty years—within the lifetime, that is, of most of the population. The men who made the bomb in 1945 hoped, as one put it, that it would blackmail humankind into keeping the peace. That hope has been realized, tenuously. But a nagging unquiet lingers beneath the surface of a world dependent for its survival on a doctrine whose acronym is MAD, for mutual assured destruction. The necessities of 1945 were mother to the invention of the bomb. We have not yet devised an answer to the necessity of our own time—a more reliable guarantee than terror against the end of the world.

THIS BOOK WAS born in shorter form as a project for *Newsweek*, a special report marking the fortieth anniversary of the bomb. Such commemoratives have become a commonplace of our journalism in 1985, a year unusually rich in targets of opportunity; it has been forty years since the end of World War II, thirty-five since the beginning of the Korean war, thirty since the conquest of polio, twenty since the reenfranchisement of the blacks in the South, ten since the fall of the Republic of Vietnam. But nothing on the calendar seems so consequential for the destiny of the planet as those days four decades ago when the atomic age began and the future of humankind was placed at hazard.

We have not attempted a formal history of the bomb, or a moral inquisition on its use in 1945 and its hegemony in the world now. "To be an honest witness," Albert Camus wrote, speaking of the narrator of his novel *The Plague*, "it was for him to confine himself mainly to what people did or said. . . ." We have tried to observe those limits in these pages. We are reporters, which is to say witnesses rather than judges. We have sought to retrieve and, we hope, to illuminate some events of our common past through the medium of lives observed—what people did and said, and what they felt, in the shadow of the bomb.

The men and women in the foreground of our story are not, for the most part, prominent in the standard works of scholarship and journalism about man's first acts of nuclear war. Their lives cannot be said to have been "ordinary," given that the bomb impinged so directly on all of them. But where a choice was available to us, we chose witnesses who had been relatively un- or undernoticed in the literature of the atomic age. They are not part of the stock company ordinarily called upon to recite in commentaries on the bomb; their testimony can fairly be said to be unrehearsed.

Their group portrait is a work of ensemble reporting by the correspondents whose names appear on the title page of this book—a journey of discovery that stretched over many weeks of pursuit and many hours of interviewing. Tracy Dahlby, *Newsweek's* Tokyo bureau chief, and Lucille Beachy, a special-projects correspondent based in New York, interviewed more than a score of *hibakusha* in Hiroshima, Nagasaki, and the United States. John McCormick, deputy chief of the magazine's Chicago bureau, sought out alumni of the team of physicists who devised the bomb, several Nobel laureates among them; his search led him to the hills of Idaho, and to the only person, living or dead, to have witnessed each of the first three nuclear explosions—the test in the Western desert and the two bombings in Japan. Martin Kasindorf, the New York bureau chief, inspected the dismantled hulk of the *Enola Gay* and talked with five of its surviving crewmen. Pamela Abramson of the San Francisco bureau found her way to the officer who had loaded the Hiroshima and Nagasaki bombs and to his stepdaughter, now a dedicated antibomb activist; when they debated the politics of nuclear weaponry for the first time in their lives, Abramson was there. Wally McNamee, a photographer assigned to the Washington bureau, contributed the pictures and his own sharp observations as well.

Our debts of gratitude are numerous. Richard M. Smith, *Newsweek's* editor-in-chief, commissioned this work and opened half an issue of the magazine to the original version. Kenneth Auchincloss, as managing editor, saw it to print with his customary wisdom and grace. Robert Rivard, as chief of correspondents, assembled the reporting team. John Whelan and Dubravka Bondulic conducted an extensive photo search in the United States and Japan. Melanie Cooper read the story for accuracy of fact and interpretation, a task she pursued, as always, with dedication, intelligence, and care. Peter J. Salber, assisted by Mata Stevenson, brought his ingenuity as a research librarian to the hunt for missing persons and vagrant bits of information; no one is better at his branch of detective work. Koko Kondo, Hideko Takayama, and Yuriko Hoshiai helped us find our way to survivors of the bomb still living in Hiroshima and Nagasaki.

We owe a special further thank-you to two particularly treasured friends and colleagues—Lynn Povich, who first thought of the idea, and Tony Fuller, who helped give it shape. This book would not have happened without them.

Others helped the metamorphosis of the work from a magazine story into a book; we are particularly grateful to Rollene Saal, who got us together with the publisher, and to Jill Grossman, who edited the manuscript. Helen Dudar, the writer and critic, read the work in progress with an expert eye, a sharp pencil, and a loving touch. She along with David Grisman, Tom Mathews, Toshiko Dahlby, Jeanie Kasindorf, Dawn Courtney McCormick, Nikki McNamee, and others close to us endured our obsession with the bomb and its consequences; our gratitude to them is great.

We are obligated as well to the men and women who agreed to be interviewed for this book, a list far longer than the six who occupy our closest attention. Some appear in the pages that follow; others have shaped our understanding of the story in ways they will recognize. Our thanks belong to them all—to Dr. Tatasuichiro Akizuki, Kenneth Bainbridge, Jacob Beser, Hans Bethe, Norris Bradbury, Jack Dairiki, Kimie Deshazo, Dr. Fumio Doko, Tom Ferebee, Mary Fujita, Takako Harada, Mary Honda, Mark Hwang, Ri Sil Gun, Dr. Mitsuo Inouye, Yoshio Kanazawa, Yun Kap-Soo, Kanji Kuramoto, Mariko Lindsey, Sister Mine Matsushita, Kay Mitchell, Akira Mukai, Ken Nakano, Sadae Nakaue, Richard Nelson, Paul Nitze, Steven Okazaki, Pak Ok-Sun, Kay Okubo, Sachiko Ota, Isidor I. Rabi, Dr. Hideo Sasaki, Yoko Sasaki, Shigeko Sasamori, Yun Kap Soo, Christiane Suyeishi, Mas Suyeishi, Jidayu Tajima, Akihiro Takahashi, Paul Tibbets, Kimiko Watanabe, Kinzo Watanabe, Robert Wilson, Suh Jung Woo, Pak Ok Sun, Yasuko Yamaguchi, Florence Yamada, Hiroaki Yamada, Ichitaro Yamada, and others.

Our largest debt of all is to the six principals in this narrative—to Billy Bryan Burns, Dorothy Douglas, Lawrence Johnston, Misao Nagoya, Kaz Suyeishi, and Theodore Van Kirk. They allowed us into their lives, their thoughts, and their memories. We hope this book expresses our gratitude to them.

New York City
August 1985

PART ONE

ZERO HOUR

1

ON A BRILLIANT summer's morning in 1945, Kaz Tanaka looked up into the sky over Hiroshima and saw the beginning of the end of her world. She was eighteen then, slender and pert, and her mind was filled with teenage things. She had wakened with a slight fever, just bothersome enough to keep her home from her job as a messenger in a war plant. But she felt well enough to be up and about, and the day stretched luxuriously ahead of her. She had even got out of doing the breakfast dishes; the August sun was already oppressively hot, and her father, who cared greatly about his gardening, had asked her to water a tree in front of their property. She ran across the courtyard and let herself out the big front gate. A girlfriend was standing across the street. Kaz waved, and the two were gossiping happily in the warmth of the morning when they heard the drone of a B-29 bomber six miles up. It was a minute or so before 8:15.

The plane did not frighten Kaz. For one thing, Hiroshima had gone almost untouched by the air war, though it was Japan's eighth-largest city and was home to a major army garrison. For another, Kaz had been born in California, and although her father had sold his produce business and repatriated to the old country while she was still in diapers, she liked to tell people she was the American in the family. The word itself had a kind of magic to her. The first time they made pictures at her nursery school, when she was two years old, she had filled her sheet of paper with scribblings in the brightest colors in her crayon box.

"What is it you're drawing, Kaz?" her teacher had asked.

"America," she had replied.

She even felt a kind of distant kinship with the B-29's that flew regularly overhead, bound north for Tokyo and other targets with their cargos of firebombs. Many people in Hiroshima called them *B-san,* Mister B, in deference to their frightening power, but Kaz thought of them as her American silver angels. *It's just the angel,* Kaz thought, squinting up into the brightness of morning; just another American angel come to see them.

She waved at the plane. "Hi, angel!" she called.

A white spot appeared in the sky, as small and innocent looking, when she first saw it, as a scrap of paper. It was falling away from the plane, drifting down toward them. Its journey took forty-three seconds.

"Oh my gosh," Kaz said, turning back to her chum, "don't tell me that's a *parachute*!" No man could be *that* brave, she was thinking, and then the air exploded in blinding light and color, the rays shooting outward as in a child's drawing of the sun, and Kaz was flung to the ground so violently that her two front teeth broke off, except she didn't know it then; she had sunk into unconsciousness.

Words failed the Japanese, trying later to describe that split-second glimpse of the apocalypse; they had to create a new one, *pika-doun,* or flash-boom, as if the nearly childlike simplicity of the term could make what had happened somehow comprehensible. When Kaz wakened from it, the world around her was as still as death.

Her girlfriend was sprawled beside her. Her mother lay pinned under the wreckage of the gate; she had come out to scold Kaz for having left it open and swinging, and it had fallen down around her, entangling her in a jumble of wood and tile. Her father had been out back tending the vegetables, working in his undershorts so as not to dirty his clothes. When he came staggering out of the garden, blood was running from his nose and mouth; by the next day, the exposed parts of his body would turn a dark, chocolate-brown, the color of broiled flesh. What had been the finest house in the neighborhood teetered crazily for a few moments at a forty-five-degree angle to the ground. Then it came crashing down in splinters, so loudly that the neighbors thought a second bomb must have fallen.

Kaz had herself been hit in the back by a flying timber and cut by shards of wood. She felt nothing. Through her numbness, she could hear voices crying, "Help me! Help me!" But people were only shapes in a dense, gray fog of dust and ash. A mushroom cloud towered seven miles over the remains of the city, a shape that would endure in the memory of mankind as the signature of a terrifying new age. Kaz never saw it. She was inside it.

2

THAT AGE HAD BEGUN for Larry Johnston in the predawn sky over New Mexico three weeks earlier, with a stab of light through a six-inch porthole in a B-29. His team had had to fight for permission to go up at all that night, and there were moments when he would gladly have been anywhere else—moments when he sat listening to the countdown tick away to zero and then empty silence. A sense of defeat swept over him, a feeling of personal failure. The two-billion-dollar doomsday machine sitting on its tower in the high desert near Alamogordo was a dud, and it was his fault. His thirty-two pieces of the puzzle had somehow malfunctioned, and had brought the whole enterprise down.

And then the darkness was ablaze from the ground to the heavens with the white light of many suns—a light so bright that, afterward, people would swear the sun had in fact come up twice that day. A single shaft pierced Johnston's side compartment, clean and brilliant, like a ray of morning in the shadows of a cathedral. There would come a time when Johnston would wish that the quest *had* failed, that the making of the bomb had been beyond human capacity. But at 5:29:45 A.M. Mountain War Time on July 16, 1945, what he felt was relief, redemption, and awe at what they had wrought—at its beauty no less than its earthshaking force.

Johnston had been part of the brotherhood that wrought it, one in a little colony of scientists and soldiers encamped on a mesa 7,300 feet up the flank of the Jemez Mountains in northern New Mexico. Their village was called Los Alamos, and it had the raw, muddy look of a Gold Rush town when Johnston first arrived in the early spring of 1944, a slender young man of twenty-six with inquiring eyes and strong, supple hands. The settlement occupied the site of what had been a boys' school, a Spartan place founded by a businessman who believed in rigor, generously laid on, as part of a proper upbringing. But in the year and a half since its discovery by the elders of the bomb project, it had become home to an astonishing community of physicists, chemists, and mathematicians, men for whom Nobel Prizes were or would be nearly as commonplace as paperweights.

Johnston had been enlisted by one of them, Luis Alvarez, his old friend and mentor, on the promise of a three-thousand-dollar annual salary and a part in a drama greater than the birth of Jesus. Johnston, deeply religious, liked Alvarez too well to take offense at his hyperbole; instead, he had laughed aloud at it. But with his initiation into the secrets of the mesa, he came to understand the underlying excitement. The men who called themselves the Manhattan Project, after their parent office in the Manhattan District of the Army Corps of Engineers, were tinkering with the mysteries of the universe and with the destiny of humankind.

Johnston was not himself one of the celebrities of the project, the frontiersmen of the mind who had created a nuclear chain reaction in a lab in a squash court in Chicago and were harnessing it to the ends of war in Los Alamos. The men whose names would become household words—the Fermis and the Bethes, the Tellers and the Bohrs—were for the most part distant figures from him and his isolated workshop. Even Oppie, the great J. Robert Oppenheimer, who ran it all, was a wraith only fleetingly glimpsed on his rounds, a thin, spectral presence moving urgently from lab to lab in worn jeans, a porkpie hat, and a contrail of tobacco smoke. He was less manager, in his bearing, than shaman, a figure of calculated mystery; he would materialize, perch on the edge of a desk, mumble some exhortations through the last glowing ember of a cigarette, and be gone.

Oppie and his immediate circle were the aristocrats of the Project, its generals, poets, and tragedians; they were quartered on Bathtub Row, a section of real houses with real tubs in a village of prefabs and trailers, and they dominated the society of Los Alamos as they would later dominate its formal histories. Johnston had neither their years nor their panache. He was a junior officer, one in a corps of bright young men conscripted from campuses around the country to make the brainstorms of their elders work. His own bent was for experimental as against theoretical physics, though the line between the two was blurring. He considered his mathematics insufficient for the highest flights of quantum theory. His particular gifts were descended instead from that older strain called Yankee ingenuity; he was happiest in a lab, working with his hands, which were one with his inquisitive mind.

He had always been a tinkerer—a threat, from earliest boyhood on, to anything that came apart. He was born in China in 1918, the son of a Princeton man who had become a Presbyterian missionary. But the family came back to America when he was five, and he was raised and schooled mostly in California. He had dissected his first alarm clock while still in rompers and had mastered the rudiments of electricity at seven or eight, with only a toy magnet, a small bulb, and a length of wire for laboratory equipment. As a sixth grader, he got curious about what made radios play. The local library suggested a book on physics. Johnston barely knew the word, let alone the mysteries it embraced. But he took the book home, and as he turned its pages, he felt a rush of discovery—a sense, as he would remember later, that he was *there*.

His further progress was not easy, in the last years of the Great Depression. There was no money; his father had been forced to abandon what had become a penniless ministry and, to Johnston's boyish embarrassment, was selling Fuller Brushes and burial plots in Forest Lawn just to put food on the table. Johnston's own formal education in science and math began modestly, in a public junior college in Los Angeles. But he learned the basics there and found his way thereafter to the right places at precisely the right time in the history of his discipline, a season of youth, innocence, and seemingly boundless discovery.

Fortune led him to the University of California at Berkeley in its days as the cradle of experimental nuclear physics in America. Alvarez was there, and Oppenheimer, already a cult figure in his thirties, and Ernest O. Lawrence, a Nobelist at thirty-eight for having invented and developed the cyclotron. Johnston sat starstruck at the weekly meetings of the Journal Club, the best and brightest of a strong department; of thirty or thirty-five people in the room any Wednesday evening, roughly a third would one day own Nobels. His passion for his calling deepened, watching his seniors at elegant play with their ideas. He wanted nothing so much in the world as to be like them.

Alvarez in turn had seen Johnston's promise and had taken him up as a kind of sorcerer's apprentice, marrying his own vaulting leaps of creativity with Johnston's painstaking experimentation. Johnston became his teaching assistant at Berkeley, then followed him to the equally heady environment of the Rad Lab, the legendary radiation laboratory at the Massachusetts Institute of

Technology. The name of the shop concealed its real purpose, which was the perfection of radar for the war, and Alvarez and Johnston had already made one major contribution to the Allied effort before Los Alamos beckoned. Together, they had devised the means for guiding airplanes home at night or in soupy weather, an ancestor of the radar-landing systems still in use today.

When Alvarez went off to New Mexico, disappearing down that black hole that seemed to be swallowing up the best minds in American and European science, Johnston stayed behind and finished the project. He had been married during his stay at MIT to a small-town California girl named Millie, and she was soon pregnant with the first of their five children. They followed his work to Los Angeles, lighting there long enough to see the blind-landing system through to production. Then Alvarez called, and Johnston, too, disappeared. Millie stayed behind in California to await the baby.

Johnston was forbidden to tell her what he would be working on, or even precisely where he would be; the encampment on the mesa hid behind the code name Site Y, and the communal address was Box 1663, Santa Fe, New Mexico, as if they all inhabited a single mail drop at the post office. Security regulations bordered on the paranoid within the wire-mesh fencing of the compound, with its DANGER signs in English and Spanish. The scientists within the perimeter were referred to formally as engineers, to blur what they were there for, and informally as the Lost Almosts, to describe their nearly total remove from civilization. They didn't even call the bomb a bomb; it was, from the moment of its conception, the Gadget—a code word chosen as if to hide its lethal potential even from themselves.

Guesses abounded among the locals as to what the longhairs on the hill were up to: building spaceships, or brewing poison gas, or, as the tavern wits had it, making windshield wipers for submarines. Johnston could not enlighten Millie, not even when he and she set up housekeeping in a green wooden four-plex overlooking Los Alamos Canyon. But she understood quickly that his work had to do with explosives—he was bringing home the cartons from detonating caps for the baby, Ginger, to play with—and she had an inkling as to what kind. Alvarez had sent Johnston a book called *Applied Nuclear Physics* as homework for their labors, and she had read it, too. One particularly suggestive passage stuck in her mind, anticipating the destructive possibilities of nuclear fission. "If the reader wakes some morning to read in his newspaper that half the United States was blown into the sea overnight," it said, "he can rest assured that someone, somewhere, succeeded."

Success was close by the time Johnston set down his bags in the dusty, nameless streets of Los Alamos in 1944, and yet still frustratingly far off. The basic questions had been answered, the equations solved; what had been born as a laboratory had become a bomb factory, and Johnston's part of the biggest, costliest, and most portentous enterprise in the history of science was to help assure that the finished product would go off.

The men on the mesa had placed their chips at first on a "gun" method—firing one piece of fissionable uranium into another to bring them to that explosive state known as supercritical mass. That contrivance proved well suited to uranium bombs of the sort ultimately dropped on Hiroshima. But it was too slow for plutonium, the stuff of what was to become the production-model atomic bomb, and there were hoots in Los Alamos at the first mention of an alternative means called implosion. The recipe was sound enough in theory: Take a sphere of fissionable material, wrap it in conventional explosives, set them off simultaneously, and compress the core inward on itself until it turned supercritical. The hard part was to make thirty-two separate detonators surrounding the sphere go off almost literally at once, within one ten-millionth of a second of one another.

George Kistiakowsky, a White Russian emigré chemist with a high IQ and a low boiling point, was head of the X (for Explosives) Division at Los Alamos and had been working on the problem without notable success when Alvarez brought Johnston around to see him. Kisty thought the solution lay in using strands of explosive Primacord, in effect as a fuse. Alvarez, seconded by Johnston, was sure he had a better idea: electricity.

"No sudden-electric detonators!" Kisty thundered. He had made the leap from sabers to atoms as instruments of war in his own lifetime, but he seemed stuck on his Primacord; ask him to evaluate electricity as a source of light, Johnston thought impatiently, and he'd probably use the time instead trying to improve kerosene and lampwick.

Johnston went ahead anyway, setting up his workbench in a sixteen-by-sixteen shack, known in Army argot as a hutment, on a lost corner of the next mesa; the others wanted him at a far and safe distance in case one of his inventions blew up. He worked with hardware-store tools, and a little gasoline-powered generator putt-putting gamely outside. He had little use for the fancier lab gear when it finally showed up, late. He had rebuilt a standard Du Pont electrical detonator cap into a working prototype with lamp cord and explosive powder within two days and was successfully testing the more elaborate finished model in six months. His enterprise overflowed his hutment into a growing cluster of buildings, a kind of mill village populated by Indian women making detonators for him.

"Well, it works," Kistiakowsky conceded. He looked as if his teeth hurt.

Johnston had by then been caught up in the supercharged life of Los Alamos, a community of scholars who worked hard six and seven days a week and played hard after dark. The frequent parties, when he and Millie went at all, interested him mainly for their intellectual ferment. Johnston was not a priggish man, but the gossip bored him, and the punch that flowed freely at socials on the mesa tasted to him like solvent; he rather preferred Sunday nights at his flat, when a crowd of believers would come around for an evening of Christian fellowship. It was the work more than the company occasions that engaged him, the shared sense that every day was Saint Crispin's Day. They were brothers together, out at the existential edge, laboring at higher intensity for higher stakes than they would ever experience again.

At the beginning, they had been driven by the knowledge that the Nazis, too, were working on the bomb; they had got a head start on the Allies, and it was thought until well along in the war that they had stayed ahead—that the most fearsome weapon in history could soon be in Hitler's hands. The fear proved ungrounded, and by the spring of 1945, the Thousand Year Reich was collapsing. But the Japanese remained, a stubborn, dangerous, and hated enemy even in retreat. The propaganda offensive against them had been as intense as the shooting war, and was sometimes tinged with racism; the President of the United States called them savages, and practically any schoolchild could recite the supporting evidence, a list of crimes and perfidies only begun by the surprise attack on Pearl Harbor in 1941. "We have begun to repay the Japanese for their brutalities," a message from the War Department instructed the scientists two days after Germany fell. ". . . We will not quit until they are completely crushed. You have an important part to play in their defeat. There must not be a let-up!"

The evidence that Japan was already teetering toward surrender did not slow the men on the mesa. On the contrary, the technological imperative had taken possession of them in their last, driven months of creation; the task had become as important to many of them as the military necessities that had fostered it. Their ruminations about the morality of the bomb, in those moments they stole from its manufacture, were made almost academic by their conviction that it was inevitable. *Man isn't through inventing things,* Johnston thought; the secret of atomic weapons was like a mountain to a climber, demanding to be mastered because it was there.

Johnston had understood from the first that it was a bomb he was working on, not some elegant laboratory exercise, and that the purpose of bombs was to blow things apart. He knew as well that the particular bomb they were fashioning at Los Alamos was one of unholy force, an instrument of death whose power could not be calculated or even adequately imagined. There was speculation on the mesa, backed by reasonable-looking equations, that it might ignite the atmosphere and light the whole world afire; at the very eve of the first test, no less a scientist than Enrico Fermi was offering bets on whether it would destroy the planet, or only New Mexico. Johnston elected to believe the theoretical boys who had calculated the risk and found it negligible; there was trust as well as inquiry in his clear hazel eyes. But he knew the Gadget was powerful enough to lift a mountain—or to end tens of thousands of lives at the push of a button.

He had never lied to himself about the consequences of what he was doing; he had in fact worried the question constantly, in thought and prayer. His commitment to his belief was not unlike that state called born-again, though he found the label an imprecise fit. He had risen at a Christian youth meeting at nineteen to confess his faith and had placed the direction of his life thereafter in God's hands. It had become his habit, in any serious matter, to present his plans to his Lord and ask, in prayer, "Is this OK or not OK? It seems to be the logical thing to do. Tell me if I'm wrong." He had made his supplications at every step in his labors in Los Alamos, and his faith, in the end, reinforced what his reason told him. Yes, the bomb would kill thousands of people, but it was ultimately a device to *preserve* life, and it was going to be built in any case, whether he participated or not.

He was accustomed to examining his feelings as carefully as he addressed his work, and he found among them a measure of personal animus toward the Japanese for their invasion of China in the 1930's. An uncle, a medical missionary there, had brought back vivid stories of their cruelty; hearing them, Johnston had thought of the childhood friends he had left behind in Shantung Province, and it was his private wish that they could know what he was doing to avenge their suffering.

But the larger end for Johnston, as for most of the men at Los Alamos, was to speed the end of a long and ugly war. The morality of bombing civilian populations was by then a closed question, each side having done it to the other; in the spring of 1945, armadas of B-29's had ignited firestorms in Tokyo, taking more than one hundred thousand lives and burning perhaps a million people out of their homes. The Americans were preparing to invade in two waves, on the island of Kyushu in November and the Tokyo plain the following March. An army of 650,000 men was being assembled, and the Japanese were digging in to resist. Their ferocity had been proven in blood on far lesser scraps of territory than their own home islands—on Guadalcanal, Tarawa, and Iwo Jima. Even schoolgirls in the Empire were practicing hand-to-hand combat with spears, and official guesses in Washington at how many GIs would die ran from the tens of thousands to a half-million or even a million.

Some of the scientists working on the bomb had

qualms about using it on people, as against putting on a demonstration drop where no one would get hurt and trying to frighten Japan into surrender. Johnston was not unmoved by their arguments. Still, there *was* a war on, a singularly bitter and bloody war, and the men in Los Alamos had become participants in it. Johnston understood that thousands of people would be killed by the bomb—he had thought and prayed hard about *that*—but thousands were already dying every day he and his associates spent at their labors. He had finally satisfied himself that their cause was just and his own course right—that the bomb would save vastly more of God's children, American *and* Japanese, than it would kill or maim.

He was accordingly "prayed-up" and prepared for what he saw the day they tested their Gadget in the desert, on a waste already so parched by sun and dust that Spanish wayfarers had named it Jornada del Muerto —the Journey of Death. They called their experiment Project TR, for Trinity, after a fancy of Oppie's; he was thought to be alluding not to the Christian but to the Hindu trinity of Brahma the Creator, Shiva the Destroyer, and Vishnu the Preserver. They raised a spindly hundred foot tower in the desert at Ground Zero and winched the first primitive ancestor of the bomb to the top, a squatty sphere of metal enclosing the secrets and the power of the universe. The elite of Los Alamos positioned themselves in bunkers ten thousand yards north, west, and south of the tower, waiting out a summer storm and glancing fretfully at their watches. Larry Johnston had a more privileged skybox seat aboard his B-29. He was part of a team put together by Alvarez to parachute little radio transmitters into the target area and measure the furies about to be loosed on the world.

The team's window into the future was a single six-inch disc of glass, and three of them were contending for a glimpse when the countdown began, the godchildren of Einstein and Hahn and Szilard and Fermi gathered to behold their inheritance. Oppie had made a row about letting them go up at all, fearful that their plane might be engulfed by the blast. Johnston's heart quickened as the seconds ticked away, but not out of fear for his life; he was experiencing something nearer the angst of an athlete or a warrior, spent by struggle, approaching the moment of victory or defeat. The seconds kept disappearing: five-four-three-two-one. Zero came and went. Nothing happened.

It's my detonators, Johnston thought. *They didn't go.*

And then the shaft of light pierced the darkness, white first, then orange. A fireball was shooting up from the ground at 120 meters a second, reddening and pulsating as it cooled; a blind girl saw the flash 120 miles away. A mushroom cloud materialized, a tower of radioactive vapor, still rising when it passed Johnston's plane at thirty thousand feet. Beneath the cloud was a space of nearly clear sky, and beneath the space, a roiling brown maelstrom of earth and rock, churning in the superheated air; what soil remained on the ground was transmuted into something new under the sun, a jade-green radioactive glass they would name trinitite. A shock wave hit the plane with a sharp thump. There was no other sound appropriate to the fury—only the dull drone of the engines in the silence of the early morning.

Some of the scientists who saw the test were stricken by it. One of them, Isidor Rabi, looked up at the mushroom cloud and felt goosebumps rise on his arms; it was, he thought, as if an ancient equilibrium in nature had been upset—as if humankind had become a threat to the world it inhabited. Some in Chicago signed petitions against loosing the monster they had created. Oppie squelched that at Los Alamos; he seemed, in the race to make the bomb, to have become committed to its use. But certitude was one of its first casualties, burned away by the fireball on the Jornada del Muerto.

"Now we're all sons of bitches," Ken Bainbridge, the test director, told Oppenheimer; it was a stinker of a weapon.

Oppie was proud of his labors; still, the words that sprang to *his* mind were a remembered fragment from the Bhagavad Gita. *I am become Death,* he thought, *the destroyer of worlds.*

Larry Johnston was too tired for introspection at that moment, and he saw no ground for penitence. He would go on to witness the bombings of Hiroshima and Nagasaki three weeks later, and would experience a tumble of more mixed emotions. The pleasure of success and the triumph of discovery would be alloyed then with trace elements of regret—not guilt, strictly speaking, but simple human sympathy. He was a physicist; he knew with some precision what must be happening on the ground to the people inside the dirty-brown swirl at the foot of the mushroom cloud. He would feel then what he imagined sailors might on sinking an enemy warship: a sense of victory tinctured by sadness that men were dying, and by the knowledge that their pain might as easily have been his own.

But he was impatient with Oppie's breast-beating over the Trinity test. Oppie had done what he believed was right, Johnston thought; they *all* had, and they ought to feel good about it. The uranium core for the Hiroshima bomb had been loaded aboard the cruiser *Indianapolis* before dawn that morning and was on its way to a speck in the Pacific called Tinian, within striking distance of Japan. Johnston himself would be following in a week, outfitted in Army suntans and faked papers identifying him as "Capt. Lawrence Johnston" to guarantee his treatment as a soldier, not a spy, if his plane went down and he were captured. He would be present at the birth of nuclear war, seeking with his instruments to reduce its terrifying possibilities to assimilable numbers.

The prospect caused him neither remorse nor shame, as it seemed to torment some of the others. He had committed offenses and unkindnesses in his lifetime, things he would always regret, but he did not count his work on the Gadget one of them. The Manhattan Project team had built a superweapon, the greatest engine of destruction in the history of warfare; it had worked, and coming back from the Trinity test, Johnston was proud. *Now we can use it on the Japs,* he thought, tumbling into bed.

Some of his fellow scientists were saying then that they might need fifty bombs to finish off Japan. Johnston, having witnessed its power that day in the desert, was an optimist; his guess was that one would do it, but either way, their brainchild was going to end the war. *On with the show,* he thought, and as he drifted into sleep, he was smiling.

3

TED VAN KIRK COULDN'T sleep at all the night they finally got the green light for Hiroshima. He thought he had retired from the shooting war in June of '43, at age twenty-two, after sixty-four missions dropping bombs and chauffeuring generals over Europe and North Africa. His combat tour over, he had hitched home, married his high-school sweetheart, Mary Jane Seasholtz, and settled into the good life in Louisiana, teaching *other* men how to navigate B-17's through flak, fire, and heavy weather. He had been idling for a year when his old flying buddy Paul Tibbets tracked him down, trying to tempt him away on some kind of secret mission; Tibbets couldn't say what it was all about, but he kept throwing around words like *big* and *important*. Van Kirk had said yes, and now it was dues time, the night of 5 August 1945, and he couldn't sleep. None of them could, so they sat up playing poker in their Quonset hut on Tinian, killing the last hours of the preatomic age.

He had a pretty good idea by then of what kind of bomb it was, though Tibbets had remained tight-lipped about it and Van Kirk was smart enough not to ask questions. He had been a chemistry buff in his school days back in Northumberland, Pennsylvania, and while he had got in only a year at Susquehanna University before the war, he had picked up enough science to know that people were doing interesting things with atoms. His suspicions grew during the long months of training with Tibbets's new 509th Composite Group; he started noticing these *nuclear* guys hanging around all the time, one of them a Harvard professor he recognized from the cover of a national magazine. Still, the word *atomic* stayed taboo in the 509th till the *Enola Gay* was airborne on its flight into history. Tibbets and the other brass spoke only of a "superbomb" that would cause a lot of damage and could end the war. Van Kirk kept his further guesses to himself.

In his discretion no less than his skill, he was perfect for his sixty-fifth mission. He and his crewmates were the Right Stuff of their day: sure, seasoned combat fliers undaunted by danger and unburdened by doubt; they were soldiers in a just war, and the bomb for them was a problem of ordnance, not of conscience. Their bloodlines were red, white, and blue. Van Kirk, the navigator, had grown up around his father's paddle wheeler, dredging coal on the Susquehanna River. Tibbets, the pilot, was born to an Illinois wholesale grocer and his wife, the former Enola Gay Haggard. Tom Ferebee, the bombardier, was a good old boy from a North Carolina farm. The copilot was a street kid from New York, the radio operator a salesman's son from Los Angeles, the electronic-countermeasures specialist an engineering student (and a Jew) from Baltimore. A Hollywood scenarist of the day might have blushed at putting together so perfect a mix.

Tibbets had in fact assembled them for their talents at war, not their demographic balance. He was unimpressed with the kid bomber crews the Air Corps was rushing into the sky in those days; he wanted men he knew he could count on, and Dutch Van Kirk had been right up around the top of his list, as cool a hand as Tibbets had ever seen under fire. Van Kirk had wanted to be a pilot himself when he joined the Air Corps in 1941, a sunny, blue-eyed stripling of twenty. He should never have passed the physical in the first place—he discovered at age fifty-four that he had been born with only one kidney—and he ultimately washed out of flight school in Oklahoma.

The reasons were unexplained at the time, and Van Kirk, in his disappointment, considered trying someone else's air force; there were British and Canadian recruiters hanging around the periphery of the base, fishing for prospects. His superiors jollied him into navigation instead. There had been a time, back in his boyhood on the Susquehanna, when his gifts for the trade might have been suspect; more than once, he had run the paddle wheeler aground in the shallows, and had heard his father shouting from below, "Don't you *know* this river?" But he showed a knack for flight navigation, enough to qualify for an accelerated training program reserved for the best prospects. He won his wings in April 1942 and graduated into Tibbets's 340th bomber squadron, then forming in Sarasota.

They shipped out that summer and flew a B-17 Flying Fortress named *The Red Gremlin* together out of England and North Africa, Tibbets piloting, Van Kirk charting the way, and Ferebee hunched over the Norden bombsight. Tibbets was the serious one, an oldtimer, by wartime Air Corps standards, at age twenty-seven, with a wife and a kid at home. Van Kirk and Ferebee liked a drink, a prank, and a game of five- or seven-card high-low for table stakes after hours. But they were all business on a bomb run. Tibbets was struck by how Van Kirk seemed to know the answer to a problem in navigation before he started working on it; if the mathematics didn't come out as he had expected, he would ball up the paper and start again. He was a perfectionist at his calculations, as Ferebee was at his bombsight, and in a tight squeeze, sucking oxygen and dodging flak eighteen thousand feet over occupied Europe, you wanted perfectionists around.

The three had their professionalism in common from the first, and combat bonded them together into something like brotherhood. Once, hunting for a German aircraft factory, Van Kirk led them to the wrong town in occupied France, and Ferebee bombed it. To the annoyance of their crewmates, they had to go back and get it right, but Tibbets even then refused to blame Van Kirk's navigation; the fault, he said, lay with the excellence of the enemy camouflage. Mostly, they were sharper and, more important for men at war, luckier. Hermann Goering's personal fighter squadron shot up the *Gremlin* one day over France, wounding Tibbets and just missing Van Kirk; he had moved his head out of the way a split second before a burst of bullets hit. They made it home.

A bomb run was otherwise as abstract for Van Kirk as banking by mail, a transaction between him and people he could not see. One of his fiancée's brothers had died on the Bataan death march, and another in the assault on Tarawa, but the war was never a personal grudge match for him—not, he liked to joke, unless someone was shooting at *him*. Neither did he let it get on his nerves as some guys did, limping in from a hairy mission and swearing, "Never again." He thought of himself as a pragmatist and a fatalist. You sat down and analyzed a problem, and if there was something you could do, he thought, you did it; after that, there wasn't much point sweating it, because it was out of your hands.

He was nevertheless eager to get home when his tour was up. The trip consisted of a series of begged rides and imaginative leaps. A mail pilot was willing, for example, to ferry him from Casablanca to Marrakech, if only there were some mail to carry there; Van Kirk scribbled off a postcard, addressed it to Marrakech, presented it to the pilot, and got his lift. Mary Jane was waiting back in the States, along with his new job teaching school. But the quiet life began to seem merely dull to him—pretty *damn* dull, he confessed when Tibbets invited him to rejoin the war. The courtship was accordingly easy. Van Kirk said yes, then took his bride to New Orleans for a last few days together. When they came home, his papers were waiting, urgently desiring his presence at Wendover Field in Utah. He hadn't even started his new assignment, and he was already four days late.

"Whoa," he told Tibbets over the phone. "What the hell's so important?"

Tibbets wasn't saying. "Take your time," he said. "Get here whenever you can."

There wasn't much *to* Wendover when the men who would make up the 509th began arriving. Their planes hadn't even been delivered yet; all Tom Ferebee saw was an American flag fluttering bravely over a single ancient bomber and an equally decrepit fighter. The nearest liberty town was Salt Lake City, 125 miles across the flats, and while a flier with ingenuity could find the leaks in the dike, it was at least nominally dry. The mission seemed as otherworldly as the billet. The aura of secrecy began with a sign at the gate: WHAT YOU SEE HERE, WHAT YOU HEAR HERE, WHEN YOU LEAVE HERE LET IT STAY HERE.

What little you *did* see or hear was hard in any case for a sensible man to credit. People in white lab coats came and went; the resident GIs called them "plumbers," on the guess that they must be tinkering with *some*thing. Some of the men had encountered the subject of nuclear physics in college and had an inkling as to what was up. Van Kirk was one, and Jacob Beser, in electronic countermeasures, was another. Beser accompanied Tibbets on a trip to Los Alamos one day, a trip so secretive they had to shed their Air Force insignia and put on Army Engineer pins instead. Mum was the word inside the compound, but with names like Bohr and Fermi floating around, Beser began putting E and mc^2 together.

"Does this thing have anything to do with atom splitting?" he asked one of the Project people, a Navy commander.

The commander laughed. "Don't ask me," he said.

Beser didn't need to. He knew he had guessed right.

The discretion was not airtight. One of the men in white coats incautiously let it slip in Ferebee's presence one day at Wendover that they were working on a "unit" powerful enough to destroy everything for eight miles around. Ferebee didn't believe him. *They're just a bunch of longhairs,* he thought. *They don't know what they're doing.*

They spent that summer and fall getting acquainted with their new B-29 Superfortresses and dropping mock-ups of the "unit" in the desert. They called the test bombs Composite B's, and some, particularly the early models, were so big and fat they couldn't be loaded in the conventional way; a young armaments officer named Billy Bryan Burns and his men had to rig up a hydraulic lift in a hole in the ground to get them into the bomb bay. In the winter, they moved to Havana and practiced long-distance flights over water from Batista Field to the Carolina coast and back—a somewhat abbreviated rehearsal, had anyone been calculating, for the round trip between Tinian and the Japanese mainland.

With spring, Tibbets tired of waiting for the plumbers to be done with their tinkering; the men were getting overtrained, and he began moving them out to Tinian a month or two ahead of the bomb, hoping their arrival would hurry the pace of science. Their life there was a warrior's torment, watching B-29's take off nightly for the Empire on real incendiary runs. The 509th was still doing practice flights once or twice a week, dropping its dummy Composite B's—or, less reverently, "pumpkins"—over unpopulated and undefended patches of land. Other men jeered them and tossed rocks at their Quonsets. Tokyo Rose mocked them in her propaganda broadcasts from Japan. Tibbets studied his flight plans. Ferebee sharpened his horseshoe game. Van Kirk waited for news of his first child, born after he had left the States. The letter that finally arrived from Mary Jane referred only to "the baby," neglecting to mention whether it was a boy or a girl. It was a boy, and they named it Tom, after Ferebee.

When their orders finally came through, Van Kirk was in the hospital with hives, but he got out in time and would have insisted in any case; he figured he could scratch as efficiently in an airplane as in bed. He shared the sense of portent they all felt, the close presence of history. Ferebee walked down to the flight line the day before the drop for a look at the newly christened *Enola Gay*. The plane was as airworthy as they came—Tibbets had picked it himself off the assembly line in Omaha—but Ferebee found it littered with bottles, condoms, skin magazines, and other detritus of men at play. It violated his sense of occasion to see the plane looking so tacky, and he got a crew to clean it up. Afterwards, he watched Captain Burns's men shepherd the bomb from the First Ordnance Squadron assembly area and load it into the bomb bay. It was leaner and more streamlined than some of the pumpkins they had been practicing with. Its nickname was Little Boy, and except for its size and the four wire antennae poking from its nose, it looked like an ordinary bomb.

It was not. At a briefing that night, Deke Parsons, a Navy weaponeer detached to the Manhattan Project, showed them pictures of the Trinity test—the fireball and the mushroom cloud—and Tibbets went over a white-knuckle turn he had worked out with Oppie to keep the plane from breaking up in the shock wave. No one was saying the magic word even then, but afterward, between insomniac hands of poker, Van Kirk leaned over to Ferebee.

"I think they're messin' around with atoms," he whispered.

"I guess tomorrow we'll know," Ferebee replied.

The flight, in the small hours of August 6, was a milk run for anyone who had dodged Messerschmitts over Europe. Taking off from Tinian in a B-29 was always a suspenseful moment, made more so for the men of the *Enola Gay* by the nine-thousand pound weight of their payload. The runway ran straight into the sea, and Tibbets seemed to some of the men to be using a lot of it getting airborne. In the cockpit, with maybe fifty yards left, his copilot was getting ready to lunge for the controls. On the apron, Billy Burns, the armaments officer, stood waving farewell. *God,* he was praying, *let him get off.*

Tibbets did, at 0245 hours, as Van Kirk noted in his log, and the rest was duck soup—a ride so smooth that they reached their target only seventeen seconds behind their flight plan. They headed north through the balmy tropical night at a sassy 4,700 feet, following the islands to Iwo Jima with their two trail planes close behind. One, *Number 91,* was coming along to photograph the damage; the other, *The Great Artiste,* bore Larry Johnston and his instruments to measure it. From Iwo, Van Kirk pointed them leftward onto a 345-degree heading, and Tibbets began the leisurely climb to 30,800 feet. Ferebee watched Captain Parsons arm the bomb, then crawled back to the nose for a nap. He was still snoozing when Tibbets finally announced to the crew that the weapon hanging from a single hook in the bomb bay was the world's first atomic bomb.

The term didn't mean much anyway, not then; not till they had seen what the bomb could do. Their mission till then might have been a training run out of Wendover. They were 150 miles offshore when Jacob Beser's instruments detected an early-warning radar signal sweeping by once and then again. It locked onto the *Enola Gay*. They were being tracked, but Beser didn't trouble Tibbets then with the news and did not need to later. The Empire was low on fighters and fuel, and a formation as small as theirs was rarely bothered.

They were still unopposed when they crossed the coast of Honshu in full daylight, easily sighting their IP —the initial point of the bomb run—in the crystalline morning air. Hiroshima lay shimmering before them, ten minutes away. You wouldn't have *lived* through a bomb run that long over Europe, Van Kirk was thinking, but there wasn't a fighter or a puff of flak in sight—only the seven-branched delta of the Ota River and the six islands that made up the city.

"I have the target," Ferebee said into the interphone.

Van Kirk wriggled forward into the nose beside him. They searched out the landmarks they had seen in reconnaissance photos, remembering the time they had bombed the wrong place in France. Everything checked.

"OK, I've got the bridge," Ferebee said, pointing dead ahead. The Aioi Bridge, one of eighty-one joining the islands, was their AP—the aiming point for the bomb. They had picked it for its unmistakable T shape. Van Kirk squinted into the bombsight, matching what he saw against an aerial picture.

"No question about it," he said. He had got them there; his job was done. They were ten miles from Zero. He went back to his seat, buckled in, and put on the welder's goggles they had all been issued, set to their maximum darkness.

Tibbets had turned on the autopilot. Ferebee was cranking data into the bombsight, correcting for an unexpected crosswind; the sight was steering the plane.

He flicked on the automatic release system. It activated an electronic tone. The men in the trail planes could hear it on their headphones.

At 0815 hours, the tone stopped. The plane jumped ten feet upward. The bomb was gone. Ferebee looked up from his sight and watched it fall through the morning, free and true, without tumbling. *Going good,* he thought. He had forgotten his goggles, and when Little Boy went off, 1,980 feet above the city and a bare 800 wide of the bridge, he felt an unbearable light stab through his eyes into his brain. *I've had it,* he thought; for a moment, he was sure the light was the last he would ever see.

Tibbets had flung off his own goggles—he couldn't see the instruments—and had yanked the wheel rightward. The plane banked dizzyingly and swung into a diving 155-degree turn. The G forces drove the men back in their seats. A shock wave rushed toward them, a tide of clear-air turbulence so violent the tail gunner could see it coming. He was yelling something incoherent into the interphone when it hit with a great *wham.* The plane lurched higher, like spindrift on an angry sea.

"Flak!" Tibbets shouted, and Ferebee was cursing the sons of bitches for shooting at them, but there were no puffs of smoke around—only a second shock wave chasing them and the voice of the tail gunner, loud and clear, bawling, "There's another one coming!" The plane reeled again, then leveled off and swung past the target for a look.

A hush fell over the crew. The city was gone.

What was left where it had been was a black, boiling witch's brew of smoke, dust, and debris. Fires were burning at the periphery, and above it all towered the cloud, less like a mushroom, Tibbets thought, than a streamer—a parachute that had failed to open.

"My God, look at that son of a bitch go," his copilot, Bob Lewis, said beside him.

They stared out at the cloud. It had risen to eye level at thirty-thousand feet in two or three minutes and was still climbing. You could look straight into it, into the twisting and tumbling shapes inside the blackness, and imagine what was happening on the ground.

Tibbets had seen enough. "What's the heading home?" he asked. Van Kirk gave it to him, and they swung southeast, bound for Tinian.

"I think this is the end of the war," Tibbets told Lewis, lighting up his pipe. There was satisfaction in that for the men of the *Enola Gay,* and in the knowledge that they had had a part in it—a soldier's pride that the mission they had rehearsed for nearly a year had been accomplished. But the scale of the devastation lingered with Van Kirk and the others, a source less of anguish than of awe, and so did the sight of the cloud; it towered behind them, a cenotaph for a city and for the innocence of the world before the bomb. They played a kind of game on the way home, a pool on how far they would have come from Hiroshima when the cloud finally disappeared from view. The tailgunner, riding backwards, was the last to see it. Van Kirk took a reading. They had traveled 363 miles.

4

THERE WAS A TOUCH of the poet about Misao Nagoya at fifteen, and as she stood under the eaves of her house near an open window, watching the bomb fall toward her, she was struck at first by its terrible beauty; it looked like a luminous silver bird floating gracefully to earth. The war had been a distant thing for Misao until that moment, though a part of her childhood had been sacrificed to it. Her family and her city had been spared, and the faint whine of the B-29's had become the object of curiosity, not of fear. But a sudden dread stole over her that morning, as she watched the single bomber and the odd silver shape spilling away from it, coming straight toward her. *It's got my name on it,* she was thinking. Time stopped. Feeling drained away. The world, for a ghostly moment, was still. *I'm going to be killed,* Misao was thinking, as matter-of-factly as if she were mastering a lesson at school. *Everyone's going to die.*

A millisecond later, she was standing inside a furnace. The earth had given a great shudder, and the heat was eddying around her, as if the air itself were on fire, and motes of dust as big as grains of rice were dancing red and orange in a fierce white light. And then Misao lay buried in the matchwood beams and the rice-paper windows of her home, the remnants of the ceiling pinning her to the floor. She raised her head a few inches and felt no pain, but a dark pool of blood was forming on the tatami mat beneath her. She struggled against the timbers for a moment, trying to free herself. In a moment more, she stopped. She had fainted. The atomic age was less than five minutes old.

The clocks of Hiroshima, those that survived the inferno, placed its beginning at 8:16; the hands froze there, as if the history of humankind till then had come to a punctuation point. At 8:15, the city had been stirring to a life at once consumed by and sheltered from the war. Men kept disappearing, children worked in munitions plants, and exhaustion had become a condition of existence for practically everybody. But Hiroshima was bound together by an unbudgeable faith in the righteousness of the emperor's war and in its outcome. The papers were full of dispatches about great and wholly fictitious victories on far-off battlefields, and when someone lost a loved one, people shrugged and said, "*Sho-ga-nai*"—it can't be helped. At 8:16, their world quite literally went up in smoke, a cauterization so complete that the living could not accurately count the dead.

Survival commonly depended on how far one was from the hypocenter, the point over the city center where the bomb went off, and Misao Nagoya was one of the lucky ones. Her family's place was 2.3 kilometers from the heart of the *pika-doun;* people within half a kilometer, a sister of Misao's among them, turned to vapor and became one with the mushroom cloud. Misao had escaped with her life, and not much more. She wakened and struggled free of the wreckage, into a world in splinters and flames. She did not know where she was or why her face and clothes were caked with blood. It would be days before she looked into a mirror and saw the cut—a deep, ugly gash that had cleft her upper lip.

The face looking back at her was barely recognizable;

the day of the *pika-doun* was the end of her childhood, and the scar was her pass into the shadow world of the *hibakusha* (pronounced, he-*bahk*-shuh), victims of the bomb. She had been a bright, spritely adolescent when the sun rose that morning, a bit unsolemn for the lock-step ethos of Japan at war. Once, a teacher had caught her and her classmates laughing and chatting when they were supposed to be cleaning up their homeroom. Misao had stepped forward, announcing that she had been responsible for the mischief. She had supposed that the others would follow her lead, but when she looked around her, they were standing silently, heads bowed, letting her take the blame alone; an empire besieged had neither the time nor the tolerance for child's play.

Still, Misao remained a daydreamer in a world grown too somber for dreaming. She developed a schoolgirl crush on Akira Yamanouchi, a leading movie heartthrob of his day, and went to all his pictures; she loved him especially in *The Navy*, cutting a romantic figure in his officer's whites. Her favorite book was an anthology of poetry, Japanese and foreign; she tried to memorize a few verses every day, and imagined herself teaching literature when she grew up.

But the reveries of girlhood, and the laughter, had fallen victim to the first total war. Misao worked four- and six-hour shifts at a lathe in an ordnance plant, cutting steel rods into bullets; her single enduring memory of the experience was that nobody ever spoke or smiled. The nearest thing to a school outing was a day on the riverbank in the sweltering sun, learning to fight with bamboo spears. An unruly corner of her mind wondered why they were doing that if the Japanese were really winning the war. But she accepted the common belief that they would—that if all else failed, the divine wind called kamikaze would start blowing and lead them to victory.

Her faith died on the morning of August 6, buried in

the rubble of her home. The bomb had ignited a firestorm at the center of the city, borne along on gale-force winds of flame; when Misao stumbled out into the day, she could see it coming toward her, the neighborhood beginning to burn at the edges like paper in a hearth. She found her grandfather, miraculously unscathed. A great wind at the moment of impact had picked him up like a bit of origami and set him down in a steeple-shaped enclosure, formed when a building beam crashed against an old stone washbasin. Everyone else was gone—her father to his job at the railyard, nearer the center; her mother to the doctor, with the baby; her seven other brothers and sisters to their war work or to the homes of relatives in the country. She assumed that only her own neighborhood had been hit—superbombs then were the stuff of science fiction—and that the others would come looking for her. She and her grandfather were afraid to stay and afraid to run, until the fire devoured the house next door; then they ran.

They pounded along, Misao in billowy *mompei* pants and bare feet. They found their way to the Ota. The bridges were gone. The banks were crowded with refugees from the flames. The wide channel was clogged with the bodies of the burned; it was hard to tell the living from the dead. Misao and her grandfather kept running. Her heart was pounding, but she couldn't stop, not until they had reached a hilltop on the edge of the city and turned to look back for the first time.

It wasn't her neighborhood alone that had been hit; all Hiroshima lay before her, a lake of fire and coal-black smoke. Long lines of people were trudging up the winding hillside roads, a spectral procession out of the holocaust below. They were women and children, mostly; the men had gone to war. They walked like somnambulists, arms thrust forward to keep their burns from brushing against their sides. Sheets of skin trailed from their fingertips. Their hair stood in spikes, held up by an impasto of sweat, dust, and dried blood. Features had been burned away; eyes had melted in their sockets, and noses and mouths had been reduced to open holes. Women's backs were marked with intricate patterns; the flash had tattooed the designs from their kimonos onto their flesh. There was no sound except the shuffle of feet and, here and there, a stifled moan.

The silence was like a shriek. Misao tried to speak and could not; she wanted to cry, and had no tears.

She didn't know if she was more than technically among the living, and if so, how long she could survive. At a point in her trek—she had lost all sense of time and place—a black rain began to fall, big, greasy droplets spotting what remained of their clothes. It was the dust and ash of Hiroshima raining back down on them, but no one knew that, and rumors coursed wildly among the dispossessed: the American beasts, having destroyed the city, were showering the survivors with oil and would set them all afire.

Misao was terrified. She ran deeper into the mountains, her grandfather still beside her. They came to a farmhouse and asked the time. It was 3 o'clock. Misao was stunned; it felt as if no more than an instant had passed since the bomb.

They went home to the city that night, hoping to find their family. Their house was in embers, carpeted over with hot ash. They found a school playground receiving the maimed and the homeless. A soldier gave Misao a ball of rice; it was half rotten, but she ate it. Flatbed army trucks disgorged their cargoes of the wounded and burned. The bodies lay on the ground like damaged goods from a warehouse. Misao and her grandfather watched but could not speak; it was, she thought afterward, as if they had lost even their identity as human beings.

She lay sleepless that night, next to a soldier bloated from head to foot with his burns. Their bodies were touching. He cried out in the dark for water. It hurt her, but she did nothing; she had been taught that water was bad for burn victims—that it might even kill them. When daylight came, her body and the soldier's were still touching. Misao looked at him. He was dead.

She went home the next morning with her grandfather and found her family. All, extraordinarily, had survived, all except her younger sister; she and six-hundred schoolmates had been conscripted to clear a firebreak a few blocks from Zero and had vanished, smoke on the air. The living scavenged among the ashes for the surviving bits of their worldly estate—a few pieces of summer clothing at the bottom of a washtub; a cast-iron rice cooker with the charred remains of their last breakfast; a cache of potatoes in a backyard storage pit, baked to a piping-hot mush. There was not much more. But Misao's father had been trained as a cabinetmaker and was clever with his hands; he fashioned a hovel that day out of odd scraps of wood, and within three weeks had built a small, tin-roofed approximation of a home.

For weeks, Misao and her mother hunted the center of the city for Misao's lost sister. Misao's own health was failing; her gums bled, her appetite disappeared, her skin turned yellow with jaundice, and she was plagued with diarrhea. She thought she was dying, but she kept on with the search; it was commanded by custom that they find *something*—a sliver of bone, a granule of ash—to enshrine with their ancestors. They moved through the city as through a dreamscape by Hieronymus Bosch, past distended bodies heaped in great piles and cremated en masse; at night, only the ghostly blue balls of flame over the corpses lit their way. Once, they came upon a concrete water tank, and Misao peered down into the muddy water. A severed leg lay at the bottom. But they found no trace of Misao's sister; when they gave up their search at last, Misao had only her life, her emptiness, and her rage.

5

KAZ TANAKA, TOO, had wakened in a frightening new world—a world whose fixed points of reference lay reduced to kindling and whose dominant sound was a silence broken only by the cries of the dying. The very air seemed hostile, so thick with dust and ash that she could barely see. She fought free of the daze cobwebbing her mind and found her girlfriend next to her.

"What happened?" they both blurted at once. There were no answers; no one knew.

"Are you hurt?" Kaz asked.

"No, I can get up," her girlfriend answered.

"Thank heaven!" Kaz said. She struggled to her feet then, bleeding from her cuts, and took her first steps onto the ravaged new terrain of her life.

That life had been a comfortable one, wanting in nothing—not, at least, until the war. Kaz's father had been born to a family of some wealth and social position in Hiroshima, and had migrated to America in the early 1920's in the spirit of adventure, not of need or flight; he never intended to stay. He had opened a produce market in Pasadena and had run it until he tired of it, doubling its business every year for four years. He moved back to Hiroshima then, at forty, for *the ancestors;* it was expected of him as the sole male heir to their name. But he brought his American baby girl with him, and a life-style flavored with American ways.

His notions of child-rearing were activist and demanding. He installed a personal playground for Kaz and her brother, but he believed in toughening them as well. He wakened them early every morning, gathered up the neighbors' children, and led them all on a mile run in their bare feet. One summer day, the street was hot enough to burn Kaz's soles, and she set out with her shoes on. Her father gave her a loud whack in full view of the other children. The shoes, at his command, came off; if Kaz ran in them, he said, she would go soft and spoiled.

The house he built, on a hill commanding a view of the Inland Sea, was a spacious one, two stories high; a row of rental properties stood like satellites across the street, testimony to his and his family's well-being. There was a courtyard in front of his place, guarded by a large, ornamented gate, and two gardens in back, one to provide vegetables, one to delight the eye in the formal Japanese fashion. A tall *butsudan,* a family altar, dominated the interior, but one of the two living rooms was American, with easy chairs instead of tatami, and so were the kitchen and bathroom fittings. Dinner was Japanese, the family sitting on the floor in the traditional way. Breakfast was American, pancakes or bacon and eggs, taken at the kitchen table.

The split vision never changed, even when war commanded their undivided allegiance to their homeland. When the news came that the Japanese had bombed Pearl Harbor, Kaz's father retired, brooding, to his garden and stayed all day, shaking his head and refusing to speak to anyone. "Pitiful!" they could hear him murmuring to himself. "Pitiful! *Pitiful!*" But he could not shut the war out of the sheltered world he had built for himself and his family. His children went to the factories part-time. His servants were conscripted for war work. Food was short; his vegetable garden became less a hobby than a necessity, helping feed not only his own household but his neighbors as well.

What remained of the life he had made was blown to bits on the day of the *pika-doun,* though his home was more than a mile from the hypocenter. He was working on the side facing Zero, and the white heat of the flash, even at so great a distance, seared the front of his body; only his loins were protected by the thin covering of his underwear. "I'm hurt, I'm hurt," he cried, stumbling out of the garden. His face was red with blood, and his flesh, when Kaz touched him, had the soft feel of a boiled tomato.

Even time seemed broken in fragments, its pieces tumbling in Kaz's mind and memory like spilled bits of a mosaic. She was setting out to look for her brother at his school nearer the center, but the streets were full of people fleeing the city, a procession of ghosts, she thought, and she had to turn back. She was on a crowded hillside, offering pickled plums from a crock that had somehow survived, and a schoolteacher was reaching out to touch its cool ceramic surface. "Please, it's so hot," the teacher was saying, and the children she had brought to the hill were crying for their mothers. Kaz wanted to help them, but when she went back the next day, the teacher and most of the children were dead.

She was walking toward her aunt's house across the city, seeking shelter, with some dried rice and some first-aid supplies in a padded bag she had rescued from the rubble. But she had gotten no farther than five-hundred meters when she was stopped by the fire, and the streams of people fleeing before it; they were jumping in the river to escape it, their live forms mingling with the bodies of the dead. Some, seeing Kaz's bag, were sure she must be a nurse and were crying out to her, "*Please*. Please help me." She came upon a person with a broken arm. The bone was sticking out through the flesh. Kaz improvised a splint out of two sticks and a length of rope and went on. She found a girl she knew, the sister of a classmate. There was a hole in her chest. Kaz wasn't sure she was still alive. She dug a piece of cotton out of her bag, laid it gently over the wound, and kept going. She passed a baby barely old enough to walk, standing unsteadily between its mother and father. The baby, naked but unhurt, was waiting for them to wake up. They were dead. Kaz kept walking.

She was at home again when a tall figure appeared, a silhouette standing where the gate had been. "He's back, he's back!" she shouted; her brother, at six feet, towered over most Japanese men, and she knew at a glimpse that it was he. But when she drew closer, she could barely recognize him through his wounds. His school had fallen down around him. His neck had been laid open, spilling blood everywhere. A friend had helped him get away. He had collapsed once, too faint to go on. A stranger had given him a swallow of sake and revived him. He had struggled on to a makeshift first-aid station. They had splashed some Mercurochrome on the open gash, tied it with a bandage, and sent him on his way; he had willed himself home from there.

For a moment, he stood swaying at the ruins of the gate, smiling at Kaz. She stared at him. His blood had congealed on his face and turned his white shirt brown. He looked as if he came from another race, another country.

"Do you have any perfume?" he asked.

"Look at this house," she said, gesturing toward what was left of it; it was a pile of boards on the ground. "How could I have any perfume?"

It was then that the smell of his blood engulfed her, as violent as the odor of a charnel house. She thought she might retch. She found a bottle of wine, left behind by a man fleeing the city. "We don't have any perfume, so *this* will be the perfume," she said. She doused her brother with it, trying to drown the stench of death.

A plane flew over, low, terrifying everybody, and close behind, the black rain fell, frightening them again. Later, when night had fallen, they moved Kaz's father into the family bomb shelter, a dugout made of heavy beams with a thick layer of sod over the top. He was a large man, and his body nearly filled the space; their mother slept in the entranceway. Kaz and her brother made for the mountains, falling into the processional of ghosts; a friend from Kaz's factory lived in a village on a hill behind the city and had offered to take them in.

It was midnight by the time they found her place. Kaz looked back. The city was ablaze. She felt a spasm of fear, not for herself but for her parents. She left her brother behind, and then she was running again, down the hillside toward the flames. The streets were clotted with the dead and the barely living, shadows backlit by a thousand fires, and a hidden sickness was sprouting like a black flower in Kaz's own body; still, she kept on running, knowing only that she had to be home.

6

FOR NUMBERLESS OTHERS, it was as if Buddha's wheel of eternity had come to a stop when the bomb went off, determining who would die and who would survive at what cost in pain or sorrow:

Yoshio Kanazawa's house was just six hundred meters from the hypocenter, but he had been bothered by a nagging summer cold and had gone out early to the clinic to see if they had anything for it. He was at the head of the line, signing in, when a brilliant white glare flashed through the building like sheet lightning. He scrambled out. The walls were falling down around him as he ran. His left hand had turned to bloody pulp, and a triangle of glass was stuck in his scalp like an arrowhead. *I've got to get home,* he told himself, stumbling out into the street. *I've got to get home.*

His way there was, for a teenage boy, a journey through a surrealist's rendering of hell. He passed the twisted steel skeleton of a railroad car, somehow still upright on its tracks. A draft horse lay by the river bank, shuddering in its death throes. The pilings of what had been a bridge poked up out of the water like rotted teeth, snagging the bodies of the dead as they floated by. *I've got to get home,* Yoshio thought, flogging himself onward, till he arrived and discovered that there was no place left to get to. His home and his family had disappeared.

In a rising panic, he searched what remained of his neighborhood and found his two elder brothers in a rude bomb shelter, not much more, really, than a trench gouged out of the ground. They were twisting and writhing in the muddy water at the bottom. Their bodies were covered nearly from head to foot with third-degree burns. Toward evening, they died. He had been one of six children in his family before the bomb. Afterward, only he was left alive.

IT HAD BEEN a long wait in the warm early morning, but the streetcar finally materialized, and Mary Fujita climbed aboard. "Boy, it's going to be hot today," she said aloud. The operator, a woman, nodded in agreement and left the door open, hoping to catch some stray trace of a breeze. Mary was turning to find a seat when the white light came, and then, as suddenly, darkness, as if the trolley had plunged into a great hole. She found herself flying improbably through the open door, hitting the ground and rolling over and over. When she struggled to her feet, the streetcar operator was beside her, her nose nearly severed by broken glass. Mary was unhurt and uncomprehending.

There had been no boom, no sound at all to suggest that a bomb had fallen. It was as if she were trapped instead in a bad dream; she thought for a time that she might even have died and gone to a different world. She passed a cigarette factory; the women who worked there were wandering naked in the street, their faces seared and bloodied, their hair burned short. She saw houses reduced to heaps of debris and heard voices crying for help; she tried to get at them but couldn't. She came upon a woman lying in the street with both legs broken. People were stepping on her in the panicky rush out of the city. Mary tried to lift her by one arm. The skin came off whole in her hand. "Come on, I'll carry you," she said, but they were separated in the crush; Mary lost sight of her and hardly dared guess afterward what had become of her.

Mary had her own family to worry about, her husband and their teenage son. She had been sent to America twenty-one years before to marry her second cousin Joe Fujita, a match made by their two families. He had emigrated earlier and was working in a sawmill in the Pacific Northwest; she was sixteen and not yet through school. With the death of Joe's father in 1940, they had come back to Hiroshima to settle the family affairs and had become part of a colony of several thousand Japanese-Americans trapped in the city by the war.

On August 6, the city's destiny became theirs, and Mary Fujita's; the bomb did not discriminate between Japanese and Japanese-Americans. As the extent of the devastation became plain to her, she was frightened mostly about her boy, Gene, who worked at an army food center. Joe would be all right, she thought. Joe had his made-in-U.S.A. motorcycle, a big Harley-Davidson. Joe could ride his cycle out of harm's way.

She hunted the streets until she found her son; he had swum the river to get away from the firestorm and was still sopping wet, but he was uninjured. Joe had vanished. In the morning, Mary and Gene went back into the heart of town with an uncle to look for him. The city was still burning; the streets were so hot you couldn't walk on them except in heavy-soled shoes. They were picking through the embers of the neighborhood where Joe should have been when they found the Harley. A body lay nearby, in ashes.

"This must be him," Mary's uncle said. The body had plainly been that of a big man, and Joe had been tall by Japanese standards.

Mary scooped up a handful of ashes, then suddenly

flung them away. "No, no!" she cried. She had spied the dead man's teeth among the cinders and had seen the glint of gold. Joe never even had to go to the dentist; his teeth were *perfect*.

Hope died hard, but at a small distance from the first heap of ashes, they found a second. The teeth once again had survived. They were white and strong. It's Joe, Mary thought. The teeth were all that remained of her husband. She picked them up and took them home.

THE GIRLS AT Hijiyama Middle School were chattering and giggling when the *pika-doun* came, a blue-white light as blinding as a summer sparkler multiplied a million times. Yasuko Kato, then twelve years old, did as they had all been taught; she covered her eyes with her fingers, plugged her ears with her thumbs, and took shelter under her desk. It's probably a drill, she was thinking, but when she lowered her hands, she knew it was not. The laughter had died, and the chatter; instead, there were shrieks of pain and fear. Faces swam in Yasuko's vision, children's faces, streaked with blood and framed in blackened stubble; the heat of the blast had burned their hair away.

The teachers herded them all outside into the yard, and the headmaster stood on a wooden box to address them, trying to explain that they had been hit by some new type of bomb. The children hardly heard his words. They were staring over his shoulder into the sky, transfixed by what they saw. A giant mushroom shape was boiling up out of the ruins beyond the school, swelling and spreading as it climbed, until it had blotted out the sun. There was something totemic about it, an aura of power and evil. The children watched it rise, higher and higher, and then they were running, seeking shelter from the cloud, ducking and dodging through the flow of refugees with their outstretched arms and their blistering burns. They were living men and women, but in

Yasuko's eyes, they were like ghosts out of the stories old people told. She was afraid to look at them.

She and her classmates took shelter at first in a little Shinto shrine on a hillock a half-kilometer away. Later, she started for home, trying to find a way through the firestorm. She couldn't, and a friend took her in for the night. In the morning, she tried again. The playground at her school was piled with bodies, the quick and the dead intermingled and indistinguishable from one another. Once, she stumbled over what she thought was a charred block of wood. It was a baby, burned black. Its mother knelt beside it, waving a fan. She was trying to cool the infant. It was dead.

Yasuko was still trying to get home when she happened upon her eldest sister, Hatsuko, twenty-five years old and married. She learned then that she *had* no home. Her family had lived only six-hundred meters from the hypocenter, and the bomb had demolished their house as easily and completely as a fist crushing a cardboard box. Yasuko's mother and another sister, Sueko, twenty-one years old, had been caught in the wreckage. For an agonizing moment, Hatsuko had stood paralyzed between the two of them, unable to choose which to help first. Flames had risen around her. She had heard her mother's cries and had seen Sueko's hair catch fire. She hadn't been able to reach either one. The heat had been unbearable. She had fled, she told Yasuko. Their mother, their father, their grandmother, and their sister Sueko had died.

Hatsuko had spent that night lying on the river bank, watching the corpses float out to sea; then, with daybreak, she had set out to find Yasuko. She had begun to vomit, as she moved through the streets, and finally had lain down to rest, unable to go on. A truck laden with bodies had stopped, and two soldiers had tried to pitch her aboard. She wasn't dead yet, she had protested, but she was in fact dying; it was as if she were an emissary from their family, Yasuko thought later, reprieved only long enough to find Yasuko and tell her what had become of the others. Hatsuko's days ebbed away thereafter in an overflowing hospital ward, a bedlam of sobs and screams. She turned inward, into a private purgatory, pursued by her guilt at having left her family to the flames. *The heads*, she muttered in her last delirium. *So many heads trying to catch me.* On the eighteenth day, with Yasuko at her bedside, Hatsuko died.

SADAE NAKAUE had wakened feeling sick, the price, she guessed, of having had too little to eat and too much to do for too long a time. There were her own three children to look after, and now a fourth, Setsuko, an unwanted girl her husband had taken in; there were as well the duties that fell to her as the wife of a Christian minister. He had come home briefly from his own morning rounds just before 8 o'clock, just long enough to poke his richly mustachioed head in the front door and ask Sadae if she were feeling any better. She had called out that she was all right, and a few minutes later, she, too, was out with her baby girl, distributing tins of tangerines to members of their congregation.

She had just delivered the last when the bomb went off in the sky above her. It was, she thought later, like something out of the Bible; a great wind rose around her, and a brilliant purple phosphorescence painted streaks in the air, the lines dancing like a road map come to unruly life. Sadae barely knew what she was doing—only that she was trying with one hand to shield the baby and clawing with the other at a shaft of wood lodged in her own right leg just below the knee. Her five-year-old had been chasing dragonflies in an empty lot. She didn't know where he was and couldn't stop to look; ropes of flame were leaping over her head, and whirlwinds churned the air around her, tornadoes of flying wood and brick.

She began limping toward City Hall, with her own baby and two lost children in tow; she could think of nowhere else to find haven. She barely made it. Blood was spurting from her leg, and by the time she arrived, the pain had become overwhelming; she could no longer walk. Some civil-defense workers offered to take her to the Red Cross hospital, but as they lifted her and her baby onto a stretcher, others of the walking wounded surged around, a human tide of suffering. They were trying to bump her aside, crying, "Take me, take me first! I'm more seriously injured than she is."

Sadae found herself lying at last on the hospital steps, one in the spillover of casualties; there wasn't enough room inside for all of them. Her husband's ward, Setsuko, had somehow found her with food and medicine and the news that her little boy was safe; the atomic wind had swept him off the ground and set him magically down in the arms of a neighbor. Sadae raised herself on her elbows to say thank you. As she did, she glanced past Setsuko at a body lying a few meters away. It was a man's form, red and bloated nearly beyond recognition. Sadae might not have known him except for the luxuriant walrus moustache. The man was her husband. He had been dead for some time.

SHIGEKO SASAMORI was only a junior-high-school student at thirteen, but even children were part of the war effort, and her class had been put to work helping to clear a firebreak about a mile from the center. She was walking there with a girlfriend when she heard the sound of the *B-san* and saw an object tumbling from its belly. "Look, something dropped!" Shigeko cried, whereupon the air turned white-hot and a great force flung her to the ground; it was as if the sky itself had fallen on her.

She passed out, and when she wakened, the light was gone; a smoky gray haze lay over the city like a fog on the sea. Shigeko had been looking at the bomb when it blew up, and her face, her chest, and her arms had been burned black by its fierce heat, even at a mile's distance. She was only barely aware of what had happened; the single thought in her mind was to run away, before the planes came again. People were surging past her through the murk, rushing outward from the center of the city toward the hills. She felt herself propelled along in the crowd like driftwood on the tide. They came to the river. Their side was on fire. They surged across a bridge, trampling anyone who fell. Flames were already licking at the bridge. It gave under their weight and collapsed behind them.

Shigeko found her way to an open schoolyard, crowded with the walking wounded. She sat down and passed out again. Someone moved her inside, into an auditorium that was still standing. She lay there for five days and four nights, floating in and out of consciousness, without food or medical care. She was homesick and scared. She would hear people moving about, and would beg them. "Please give me water. Please tell my parents."

On the fifth day, her parents came; she could hear her mother calling her name. "Here I am," she answered. Her voice was small and weak, but her mother heard it and took her home.

Shigeko's face was black and swollen, its features lost under the charring; her mother told her afterward that they couldn't tell the front of her head from the back except by looking at her body to see which way she was facing. They cut off the singed remains of her hair and the charcoaled outer crust of skin. It had become infected underneath. There were no doctors and no medicine. Shigeko's parents were sick themselves from radiation, but her mother sat beside her all day, laving her burns with soybean oil, and slept next to her at night. She could barely eat—her mouth was burned inside—and she was unconscious much of the time. Her mother listened often to her chest to see if she were breathing; it was as if she were *expected* to die.

That she survived at all, she supposed later, owed to her mother's will and God's power; it was inexplicable to her except as a miracle. Its cost was great. Her mother had been reassuring during her long, slow recovery; she had promised Shigeko that her scars would heal and her skin grow back as good as new. Shigeko was naive; she believed it, until the day she saw herself in a mirror. She was shocked by the apparition looking back at her—the face, she thought, of a monster. Her skin was red, and the heat of the bomb had burned away the flesh beneath it. Her eyes bugged out. Her nose, once flat, was a protuberance of skin and bone. Her mouth hung open, the lips distended. She knew how different she looked the day she went outside for one rare time and was surrounded by children calling, "Hello! Hello! Hello!" They were trying out their bits of GI English; she had been so transfigured by the bomb that they thought she must be American—one in the alien race that had dropped it.

YOKO SASAKI, in her teens, was walking along toward the doctor's office with an earache when a little family tableau caught her eye: a young mother holding up a baby to wave bye-bye to its father as he left for work. Then came the flash, as if the sun had fallen to earth, and suddenly the young man was alone. His eyes were blank and uncomprehending. The skin of his arms dangled loose at his sides like curling parchment. His house, his wife, and his baby had disappeared.

Yoko held her own arms out, the posture of the *hibakusha*. The skin was shredded, the flesh exposed and raw. *Those arms look burnt*, she thought, as if they belonged to someone else. She fainted.

When she came to, her mother and her sisters were carrying her to an air-raid shelter on a makeshift litter, a

Asahi Shimbun

EXPLOSION OVER HIROSHIMA: The signature of a terrifying new age.

Tom Ives

ZERO HOUR: A watch stopped by the blast.

THE *ENOLA GAY:* Dismantled now, the plane will be restored as a museum piece.

Los Alamos

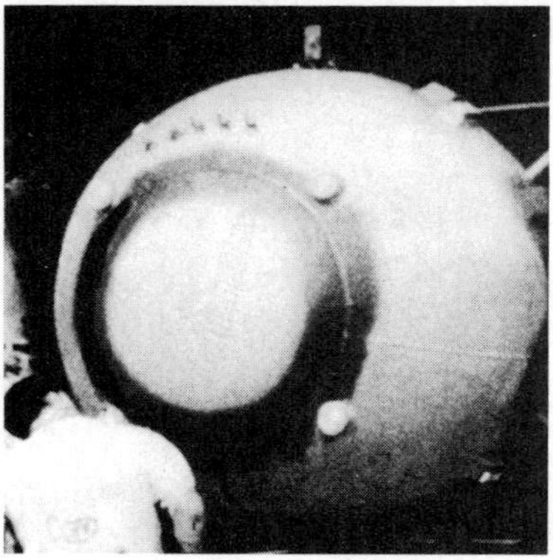

Los Alamos-CBS News

FAT MAN: It missed its aiming point by nearly a mile and a half but leveled nearly half of Nagasaki.

THE RUBBLE OF HIROSHIMA: In a place reduced to a desert of ash, the living could not even count the dead.

Shigeo Hayashi

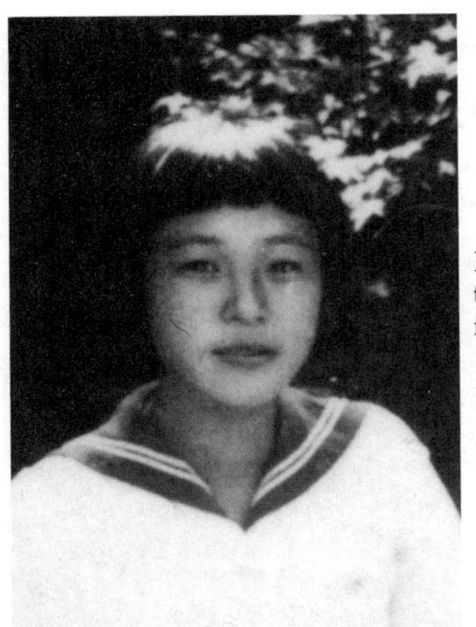

KAZ TANAKA: She never saw the mushroom cloud—she was inside it.

KAZ TANAKA SUYEISHI IN LOS ANGELES: "You, me—brother, sister. I don't hate you."

Wally McNamee

LARRY JOHNSTON ON TINIAN: He knew the Gadget could lift a mountain or kill tens of thousands.

LARRY JOHNSTON IN IDAHO: There was no way the bomb could have been stopped from happening.

Wally McNamee

NAVIGATOR "DUTCH" VAN KIRK: A hush fell over the plane—the city beneath them was gone.

TED VAN KIRK IN CALIFORNIA: It was a job that had to be seen in the context of its time, as an act of war intended to end a war.

Wally McNamee

MISAO NAGOYA WITH HER BROTHER: "I'm going to be killed. Everyone's going to die."

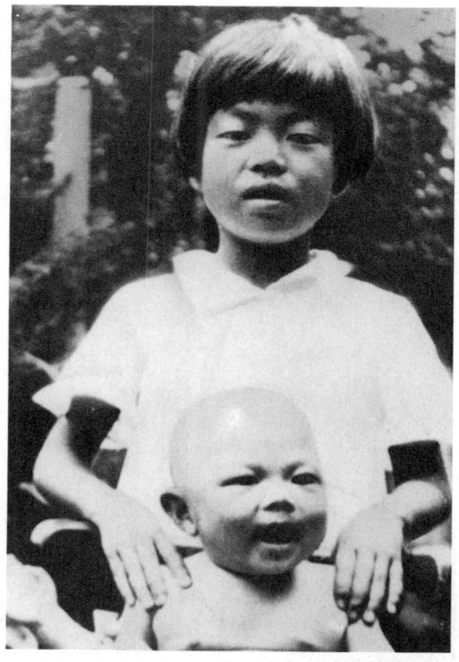

MISAO NAGOYA AT PEACE MEMORIAL PARK IN HIROSHIMA: Anger was her armor against suffering, her medicine for her own ill health.

Wally McNamee

ARMAMENTS OFFICER BILLY BRYAN BURNS: He did not regret loading the bombs—they had been weapons in a righteous war.

DOROTHY DOUGLAS AND HER STEP-FATHER BILLY BRYAN BURNS IN NORTH CAROLINA: She saw the bomb as destructive of life, whereas he saw it as saving lives.

Wally McNamee

Wally McNamee

FORTY YEARS AFTER THE BOMB: Hiroshima rises from the ashes.

cedar rain shutter salvaged from the ruins. The shelter was a catacomb of pain, its silence rent by wailing and crying; Yoko could hear someone begging to be put to death. Her own body was nearly half covered by burns, and her consciousness of what was happening to her was swallowed up in her suffering. She was somehow at her aunt's house. Her mother was daubing her burns with machine oil—there was nothing else. Her little sister, two years old, was begging for water. Then she was dead; their uncle carried her tiny body away in a bureau drawer for a coffin and brought her ashes home in a teacup.

And then Yoko herself was dying. A doctor came one day and looked at her; afterward, she could hear his voice at a great distance, telling her parents gravely that she had no more than a few hours left to live. She looked up. He was hovering beside her, drawing a white cloth over her face. "I'm very sorry," he said. Yoko couldn't see, or move, or even form a single word, but she felt something inside herself harden, some reserve of will beyond the ken of medicine. *I will never die,* she told herself. *I will never, never die.*

7

THEY SAT IN Oppenheimer's office in Los Alamos, Oppie and Hans Bethe and some of the other eminences of the Manhattan Project, watching the first films of the destruction of Hiroshima. The lights were out. The shades were drawn. The room was dark. No one spoke. The only sound was the chatter of the projector. Grainy images flickered on the screen, autopsy pictures, taken from the air, of a city that had died.

Bethe, in the silence, felt emotions he had never expected—alternating waves of shock at the damage and pity for its victims. He was a half-Jew who had fled Europe a step ahead of the Nazi tide. He had run the theoretical division at Los Alamos and had been a willing participant in the making of the bomb, even when it seemed possible that his own father back in Germany might die of his contrivance; to have let Hitler beat the allies to it would have been to sentence Western civilization to return to the Dark Ages. Bethe had known, as a man of science, what the bomb would do, and the devastation he saw on the screen was not greater than he had calculated it would be. Still, he thought, actually to *see* such a thing—a bomb like that must never be used again.

Bethe was not alone in his misgivings. "One of our units has just been successfully dropped on Japan!" the public-address system at Los Alamos had blared when the news first arrived, and there was dancing and drinking on the mesa that night. But some of the scientists were prey to more mixed feelings in the days that followed, their pride of authorship spoiled in varying degree by a sense of complicity in perhaps a hundred thousand deaths. Oppie would say later that they had known *sin,* and that mankind would curse the name of Los Alamos if its invention became part of the accepted weaponry of future wars. Even the men on Tinian were not wholly immune to doubt; some of the fliers Billy Burns mixed with at the officers' mess had seen the pictures from Hiroshima and were saying they didn't want any part of anything like that.

But Dutch Van Kirk shed no tears of remorse, and neither did Larry Johnston. It had crossed Johnston's mind, looking down from the side-scanner's compartment aboard *The Great Artiste,* that there was something unsportsmanlike in his safe remove from the death and devastation on the ground. He got gooseflesh, watching it; it was pretty ugly down there, and he felt saddened for the people in the middle of it. The peace of his conscience was otherwise undisturbed. The mood on the plane, among soldiers and scientists alike, was congratulatory; the Gadget had worked. They autographed one another's short snorters, the banknotes people signed and collected as souvenirs of the war; along with their names, they scribbled the words *Hiroshima Express.* The issue under discussion, as they flew south toward Tinian, was not the morality of what they had done but its utility—whether Japan would now surrender, or whether they would have to drop the other shoe.

The question was one for higher civil and military authority, not for fliers and physicists, and their answer was inevitable. The war was a brutal one before the bomb, a *total* war in which more than fifty million people, soldiers and civilians, had died. The slaughter was still going on. America had the weapon, now proven in combat, that could stop it. They couldn't *not* use it; it was there. A second bomb, called Fat Man for its chubby shape and its five-ton weight, had already reached Tinian; the cores for two more were to leave the States on August 12, and others were coming on line—perhaps as many as sixteen, Oppie had estimated, by mid-November.

The Japanese appeared to have rejected an ultimatum from Washington; in the view of the men managing the war, they had to be made to think it was going to *rain* atomic bombs until they surrendered. There was Stalin to be impressed as well; as the revisionist histories of a later generation would argue, a number of civilian leaders in the Truman administration saw advantage in using the bomb not merely to end the fighting but to assert America's authority in the postwar world. The motives that led to the first drop dictated a second, fast. With Hiroshima still smoldering, a new mission was scheduled for the ninth, and a new target list drawn. Kokura was first. Nagasaki was second.

Johnston accepted the choice and volunteered for the trail plane again. Alvarez didn't want to risk his scientists a second time; he thought a team of Army technicians could handle the measuring devices.

"Luis," Johnston said, "I hate to tell you this, but I don't think any of them are really trained to do the thing I've been doing."

Alvarez relented. "I guess you'd better go," he said. "If you don't mind."

Johnston didn't mind at all. On the eighth, he watched Burns's crew load Fat Man onto the lead plane, *Bock's Car*. Some of the men were scribbling messages on it. The second bomb, unlike the first, already bore Johnston's scientific signature; it was an implosion model, and its detonators were his work. Still, as he watched, he felt old memories wakening, of his boyhood in Shantung Province and the friends there who had fallen under the heel of the Japanese. He stepped forward with the others, tugging a pencil from his pocket. "To the people of Japan," he wrote, "from my friends in China."

The flight of Fat Man seemed governed by Murphy's Law: What could go wrong did. First, the observation plane missed connections with the others; *Bock's Car* and *The Great Artiste* had to circle the rendezvous point, wasting time and fuel. When they arrived over the Empire, their primary target, Kokura, was socked in by weather. They made three runs looking in vain for an opening; by the time they gave up, the ack-ack batteries on the ground were targeting them instead, rocking the planes with bursts of flak. The weather was only marginally better over Nagasaki, and the *B-sans* arrived with barely enough fuel left to make a single pass. They let Fat Man fly through a fleeting break in the clouds, then ran for Okinawa, the nearest place they could land. The bomb missed its aiming point by a mile and a half.

It hardly mattered; nearly half the city was destroyed, and more than thirty-five thousand people died. In a boarding house in the middle of town, Sachiko Ota, a newlywed of eighteen, was standing on the stairs with her landlady, talking about the newspaper accounts of the "new-type bomb" the *B-sans* had dropped on Hiroshima. The news had filled Sachiko with dread, and an air-raid alert that very morning hadn't helped. She had been home alone at the time—her husband was on duty as a guard at the Mitsubishi shipyards—and she had had to go off to the shelter without him. It had been a false alarm; the all-clear had sounded after forty minutes, and Sachiko had gone home. But a general alert remained in effect, and the feeling of panic had not left her. Together, she and her landlady had stuffed a shoulder bag with food, medicine, and bandages, preparing against doomsday.

They were talking about the first bomb when the second fell away from *Bock's Car* at two minutes past eleven in the morning. There was no *pika-doun* so far as Sachiko could remember afterward, no flash she could see or boom she could hear. She was aware only that the stairs, the house, the landlady, and the light were inexplicably gone, and she was lying in a flaming pyre, her nose and mouth plugged with dirt. *This is what it feels like to be a corpse,* she was thinking. She could feel the heat closing round her, but she could not struggle free, not at first; her arms were tied up in the strap of her kitbag. She gnawed through it with her teeth, then began digging out. Her landlady's voice assaulted her ears, crying for help. Sachiko could not get near her through the tangle of blazing beams.

Instead, she was running, a step ahead of the inferno. The air-raid shelter in her neighborhood was filled to overflowing with burn victims. She started for her mother's house on the outskirts of town. The dry summer grass was bursting spontaneously into flame around her, and when she stepped on a pumpkin without looking, her foot went through it; the heat wave had baked it to a soft pulp. She made it to her mother's place, numb with pain, fatigue, and grief for her husband. She had seen the sea of fire stretching from their hillside to the shipyards and could not imagine that he had survived it—not until he appeared in the doorway the next day, smiled his lopsided smile, and said, in tender surprise, "Oh, you're still alive, are you?"

Life often was all that remained to the survivors in a world turned upside down. Jidayu Tajima was in sick bay with dysentery at the Fukuoka No. 14 POW camp, where he worked as a guard and general factotum. A prisoner had just brought him a bowl of rice gruel, and he was lifting it to his lips when the building came down around him. He would never know how he escaped, only that he had; when his mind cleared, he was fleeing to the mountains with sixteen of his prisoners. They made a motley company, Japanese, American, British, Dutch, Indonesian, and Australian, but they had become one with each other and with the people they helped along the way; as Tajima would reflect many years afterward, the democracy of the bomb had made *hibakusha* of them all.

8

SIX DAYS LATER, Dorothy Burns's mom took her to the movies in Brooksville, Florida, to see *Bambi.* The picture was a sad one, and for a six-year-old girl, a little scary; there was a scene where the humans set the whole forest afire, and all the animals were running through the trees, trying to get away from the flames. Then the lights went on, and a man's voice came over a loudspeaker, saying, "Ladies and gentlemen, the war with Japan has ended." People clapped and cheered, and Dorothy's mom gave her a great big hug. She told Dorothy it meant her daddy would be coming home.

Dorothy had lost her real father the March before the war, when she was only two. He was a Navy flyer, and he was killed when two planes crashed in the air off the coast of Hawaii. Dorothy's mom, Helen, was a widow at twenty-two. They moved back to Brooksville to be near her parents, and she got a job as a secretary at the Air Corps base there. She went to a dance one night and saw a young officer named Billy Bryan Burns. He was handsome, and she was beautiful. The band was playing "Begin the Beguine." He asked her to dance, they fell in love, and in the summer of 1943, they were married.

Dorothy was in love, too. Billy had lost his own father

when he was three and had been raised by a stepfather, a newspaper reporter in Florida; he in turn adopted Dorothy—Dottie, he called her—and loved her as if she were his own little girl. He had certain ideas about things, old-fashioned ideas about right and wrong and God and family, and about winning. He liked to say there was nothing else *but* winning; winning was the whole ball game. That came from his days as a high-school baseball player, and it said something about why he hadn't gone on to play pro ball, even though the Detroit Tigers had their eye on him. Billy grew up in hard times, and he believed in thinking ahead. He *wanted* to play ball, but he put it off and went to college first at the University of Florida; to win in life, you needed a college education.

He was a lieutenant in armaments when he and Dorothy's mom first met. He had gone straight from college into the Air Corps in 1942, hoping to be a pilot, but there wasn't a slot for him, so he shrugged off his bad luck in that way he had and learned his new specialty well. Dorothy didn't know much about his work, except that there was a war on and he had something to do with it. The war mostly meant that she couldn't live with her parents. Until Billy was sent away to someplace called Wendover Field, she got to spend weekends with them in a big old house in town, with columns in front. But during the week, she stayed with her grandparents on a little farm while her mom and daddy worked at the base. She grew up with chicks and cows and calves and pigs and the smell of baking bread, and the drone of a radio in the dining room tuned in to news of the war.

She would see her daddy in his uniform in those days, and breathe the leathery smell of his jacket, and play catch with him in the yard, and she would think of the war as something bad happening in some other country far away. But sometimes he brought it home. Once, he came in from the base in a daze. Dorothy was sent to her room, but she listened anyway; it turned out one of his men had walked into a propeller and got his head cut off. There had been a scene another night at dinner; they had roast beef, and her daddy got upset. Dorothy found out later that a plane had crashed and burned at the base, and he had had to identify some of the charred bodies.

Dorothy herself learned the mysteries of birth and death as farm children do, seeing the life cycle happen all around them. Grown-ups said the stork brought babies, but she watched her dog Agnes have a litter of puppies, and she knew better. She found out about death, too. The man who brought the feed gave her some bunnies for pets. She loved them, but one night she took them to bed with her, and when she woke up in the morning, they had all smothered. That evening, sitting in a hammock under a clear night sky, her grandmother spoke to her gently about it, explaining the fragility of life and the finality of death.

She was only five years old then, too young to understand that her grandmother might be preparing her against the possibility of a death in their own family. Billy Burns had been transferred to Wendover, taking Dorothy's mom with him. But not long after the bunnies died, her mom came home to the farm, and her daddy went away to the Pacific. They didn't know where he was or what he was doing—only that it was something important. They had to wait till the war was over to find out that he had been on Tinian and that his mission had had to do with the atomic bomb.

He came back to them six weeks after V-J Day, with a Bronze Star and the insignia of the 509th Composite Group stitched to his leather jacket. The three of them moved into a pale pink house in West Palm Beach, enjoying the postwar novelty of being together. The war was over for them, and Billy didn't talk much about it, or about the bomb. Sometimes, he would cry out in the middle of the night, and Dorothy's mom would say, "Daddy's just having nightmares. It's because of the war." He did not remember the dreams, and did not regret his part in the summer of the bomb, loading Little Boy and Fat Man and waving them off for Japan. They had been weapons in a righteous war, only mathematically worse than some conventional blockbusters he had handled, and when he heard that the second had blown away half of Nagasaki, all he had been able to think was, *God, I'm going home.*

PART TWO

FORTY YEARS ON

9

FOR MANY YEARS after the bomb, Misao Nagoya lived on her anger. Anger was her armor against suffering, her medicine for her own ill health, her solace for the loss of a son. She trained it first on the Anglo-Saxon beasts, as she had been taught during the war, and then on the Japanese for having submitted so easily and completely to them. It made her boil inside, in the years immediately following the surrender, to see her own people doing the jitterbug, listening to boogie-woogie records, and imitating the fashions of their conquerors. The Land of the Gods lay under the heel of the Americans and seemed to want nothing so much as to please them. It was as if Japan had fallen victim to a case of collective amnesia. But Misao had not. She nurtured her anger, like a flower in a desert, and years later bore public witness to it. She thought she could not bear even to *meet* an American. She knew she would never forget.

She remained a handsome woman forty years after the bomb, at age fifty-five, with square, expressive features set off by steel-rimmed glasses; her hair, cropped short, was peppered with gray, and a front tooth was framed in gold. She lived with her husband in a new house on the outskirts of Hiroshima, a pretty place with a garden pond gurgling just beyond the rice-paper doors. A color picture of her first grandchild, a healthy year-old boy, occupied a place of honor on a table. But the Hiroshima schoolgirl of fifteen still dwelled beneath the comfortable surface of Misao's middle age, a teenager clawing out of the rubble of a city and wandering its streets in search of a sister who no longer existed. Her childhood had died in the white heat of the bomb, and her health, and her dreams.

She was not one of the maimed among the *hibakusha*, the people moving through the shadows with their burn scars, trying to avoid the children taunting, "*Pika-doun! Pika-doun!*" It was her life that was disfigured by the bomb. Radiation had ravaged her body, leaving her easy prey to illness all her life. She was tormented by diarrhea for nine years after the war, and her liver was so damaged that, at forty-nine, she was told she had no more than five years left to live.

Her girlish fancies of teaching literature had been just as surely a casualty of the war. Even high school had become a luxury in the poverty of postwar Japan. She had only tattered hand-me-downs to wear to her classes and had to stay home when it rained, for want of a coat or an umbrella. She managed to finish anyway and to pick up some secretarial skills. Her formal education ended there; college was out of the question.

She found a decent job instead, clerking for the railroad workers' union, and a man who loved her enough to propose marriage even if she were a *hibakusha*—a brand survivors wore as abashedly as if it were the mark of Cain. His name was Kenzo, and he was at Hiroshima University, preparing to be a social-studies teacher, when they met. It was, in a sense, the bomb that brought them together. He was a student delegate to one of the first big antinuclear rallies in the rebuilt city of the dead, and her union was among its sponsors.

She found herself drawn to him immediately; he was

not himself a *hibakusha,* but he had a sensitive spirit, and he seemed to understand the travail of the survivors of the bomb. As their relationship deepened, they began to speak of marrying, and of the social barriers they would encounter if they did. There were stories in the papers almost daily about babies being born with hideous deformities, the mark of the *hibakusha* carried to a second generation. Were the stories true? They didn't know. Would Kenzo's family resist? They had to find out; custom commanded it.

Kenzo's parents were cool when he brought Misao to his home village on Tanega-shima, a remote island off the southern coast of Japan, to seek their blessing. They received her in the hearty style of the countryside, serving her bounteous bowls of rice at mealtimes and making a fuss about how little she ate. They took the delicate state of her system as evidence that she could not bear children well, and they said so openly, reinforcing the dread in Misao's own heart. Most men would have yielded before the opposition of their families. Kenzo shrugged it off. His parents were too far away to do anything, he said when he and Misao were safely home in Hiroshima, and in 1954 they married.

Still, Misao harbored her own secret fears about having children, and when her first son, Yoshiki, contracted polio at two, she blamed herself. It did little good for doctors to assure her that there was no connection between his illness and her exposure to the bomb. Guilt was itself pandemic among the *hibakusha,* and she couldn't help believing that, after ten years in poor health, she had passed on some crippling weakness to her son.

Her anxieties were eased when Yoshiki recovered, and a second son, Fumiki, arrived in squalling good health in 1960. Fumiki was a bubbly, rambunctious boy until, one day when he was four, he quit eating. A teacher at his day-care center called Misao about it. She took him to the family doctor. He thought it was only a cold at first, nothing to worry about. But Fumiki's weight dwindled, and his coltish energy with it, and then his joints began to hurt.

Misao put him in the hospital for tests. One of the first showed that his spleen was enlarged. She didn't need to wait for the rest of the results. *My God, he's got leukemia,* a premonition told her. She was right.

Once again, the doctors tried to assuage her guilt. The incidence of leukemia, they insisted, was no greater among the offspring of *hibakusha* than in the general population; a generation of statistics proved it. But Misao could count; of five other children in Fumiki's ward, all leukemia patients, four had *hibakusha* mothers, and she took Fumiki's illness as a judgment on herself.

He was in the hospital four times over the next two and a half years, each stay longer and costlier than the last. The government at the time provided medical aid to *hibakusha,* but not their children. Misao had to keep working to help pay the bills; her life became a round of days at the office and nights at the hospital, sleeping upright in a chair at Fumiki's bedside. His illness strained the family's budget, and her nerves, and sometimes she was cross with him. "It's not *my* fault I've got leukemia," he would say, adding to the sum of her self-reproach. She knew perfectly well whose fault it was, or thought she did; she had placed her own son under a sentence of death the day she gave him life.

When there was no more money, a doctor suggested a way out: placing Fumiki in a research program studying the effects of radiation on the children of *hibakusha.* His treatment, if she said yes, would be free; the price was signing a paper authorizing an autopsy if he died. *I don't want to make my son a guinea pig,* she thought, but there was no choice; she signed.

She had little more recourse when a team of American doctors came around to examine Fumiki for their own studies on radiation. She hated them for what she saw as their hypocrisy, feigning interest in their victims, and yet she could not say so; the Japanese doctors might withhold treatment if she did. So she bit her tongue and, on August 23, 1965, confided her anger to her diary in verse:

Doctors of Japan, doctors of the world,
Please, please cure my son's leukemia.
But not you Americans.
Don't you touch my son with your hands,
Don't you touch my son with your fingers.
With your peace lovers' faces,
With your dirty hands,
Don't you touch my son.

Misao's vigil lasted two and a half years more, and all the while her bitterness grew—at the Americans for having dropped the bomb; at the Japanese media for turning Fumiki's illness into a tabloid tearjerker; at the thoughtless grown-ups standing outside the sickroom door, talking in hushed but audible tones about the poor little children with leukemia. Fumiki was not deaf; he seemed to Misao to understand the gravity of his illness. "I want to live just a little longer," he would tell her. His wish was not answered; at 2:45 in the morning of February 22, 1968, in the children's ward of Hiroshima University Hospital, he died. He was seven years old.

For more than a year, Misao stayed home and cried, her anger now turned inward on herself. *My in-laws were right,* she thought; they had warned Kenzo not to marry her, and their forebodings had come true. It was as if she were entombed in her guilt. She was sorry that she had ever borne Fumiki. At low ebb, she wanted to die.

She outlived her own death wish, and the prophecies of her doctors that it would be granted; it had been six years, in 1985, since they had given her five to live. Her sorrow had never ended. For several years, she spoke to Fumiki as if he were still alive. The conversations stopped, but even then, she knelt each day at the family altar, lit a stick of incense in his memory, and rang a small bronze bell; its resonant tone was thought to attract the notice of the spirits in the netherworld. She still felt Fumiki with her in her waking hours, sometimes as a presence in the background watching her, sometimes as a spirit filling her own person from head to foot; when she tasted something sweet, it was as if he were sharing it with her. She still saw him almost nightly in her dreams; he was always seven, always well, and always in high boyish spirits.

What Misao learned, finally, was a way to live with her pain; it was her anger that rescued her from it. The press made much of Fumiki's death, and the stories brought down a flood of recrimination against her from other *hibakusha*. They had accustomed themselves to living in silence, hiding their own shame, and now she was drawing attention to their children. Employers would be wary of them; boyfriends and girlfriends would run the other way. Couldn't she have left well enough alone? At first, she wished she had. She felt she must have done something wrong, and she withdrew more completely than ever from the world, into the cloister of her grief.

But she began in her solitude to believe that the story *had* to be told—that she belonged to a last, dying generation that could speak firsthand about the bomb and that she was *obliged* to do so. A spark was struck the day she watched the news on television and saw pictures of women and children burned by American napalm in Vietnam—the same Americans who had set her own city afire with their bomb. She plunged into the work of the peace movement, driving herself even when she felt too ill to be out and around. She collected signatures on petitions, interviewed other *hibakusha* about their suffering, and helped assemble a series of memoirs of the bomb.

She had been educating herself about the war for years by then and had come to see that her own country was not blameless in what had happened, to itself and to her. But it had been an arduous process, unlearning what she had been taught as a schoolgirl. Her response when Kenzo had first spoken to her about Japan's own transgressions against the peace in the 1930's had been an almost reflexive unbelief. "How do you *know* Japan invaded other countries," she demanded. "if you weren't there on the spot?"

With time, her understanding deepened, and she began to feel she and her generation had been brainwashed. *When we were told to turn right,* she thought, *we turned right; if we were told to turn left, we turned left.* She spoke often to student audiences on her rounds and worried that they, too, were falling victim to a follow-the-leader psychology. It became an insistent part of her message that they must think for themselves. Her best evidence was her own life.

She did not absolve the Americans of her hard judgment on them. The war in Vietnam seemed proof enough to her that they had not changed as a nation since the summer of the bomb. But she *did* meet an American one day, a young black GI on leave from the fighting. Someone had brought him to a rally at Peace Memorial Park, the leafy common marking the hypocenter of the blast, and he listened intently to several of the *hibakusha,* speaking of the damage to their lives. "Today," he told them afterward, "I too became a *hibakusha.*"

The survivors were touched by his sympathy. Afterward, he moved among them, shaking hands, till he and Misao stood face to face. His hand was outstretched toward her. She stared at it for what seemed to her a long time. Then she smiled and shook hands.

10

SIX WEEKS AFTER the end of the war, some of the crewmen from the *Enola Gay* flew back to Japan to look at what the bomb had done. Dutch Van Kirk was aboard, and Paul Tibbets, the pilot, and Tom Ferebee, the bombardier, and some of the Manhattan Project people, come as students and sightseers this time instead of warriors. They spent a couple of days on the ground in Nagasaki, staring at steel girders bent to hairpin angles and railroad ties reduced to neat lines of ash. People in the streets, seeing their wonderment, waved a single finger at them—*one bomb! one bomb!*

They never touched down at Hiroshima, though it had been their own target, and had no desire to do so. They flew over low instead, at a sheltered distance from the survivors. The three fliers had seen bombed-out cities before, but nothing quite like the wasteland beneath them—a few shells of buildings standing gutted in a desert of ash. *One bomb,* Van Kirk was thinking. *How could all this be done by one bomb, one plane?*

The plane lay dismembered forty years later, in two storage buildings in Suitland, Maryland, awaiting restoration by the Smithsonian Institution as a museum piece. The name *Enola Gay* survived in faded black paint near the nose, and a roster of the Hiroshima crewmen, Tibbets among them, and Ferebee, and "Maj. Dutch Van Kirk." The aircraft had retired from the stage of history, and so, happily, had Van Kirk. He became *Ted* Van Kirk again, shedding his nom de guerre along with his wings, his khakis, and his memories of his moment in the annals of war. "He doesn't talk about the atomic bomb very much," Elena Sanderson, his secretary at a Du Pont sales office in the San Francisco suburbs, announced firmly to a visitor. "In fact, he says he doesn't *care* to talk about it."

The office was the last post in Van Kirk's thirty-five years with the company. He had passed, in his twenties, from the military to the social history of America, one in a generation of men who came home from the war and built an affluent new society on the rubble of the Great Depression. They studied on the GI Bill, took wives, made babies, bought tract houses, drove station wagons, coached Little League, voted for Ike, and sought the well-paid security of life in large corporations. There was a time early in Van Kirk's career when he was based in the South and, as he would reminisce long afterward, his connection with the atomic bomb opened a lot of doors for him; he figured he must have spoken to half the Lions and Rotarians in Dixie. Otherwise, by choice, he was just another guy on the ladder, trying to keep moving up. The kid who navigated the bomb to Hiroshima had become the prototypical Organization Man.

He and his buddies from the *Enola Gay* had come home conquering heroes after the war. *Life* magazine threw them a party in New York, and the movie stars gawked at *them*. Tibbets and Ferebee had elected to stay in the Air Force. Van Kirk *had* to for a year; the three of them were assigned to the further testing of the bomb at a Pacific atoll named Bikini in 1946. But their celebrity was held against them; other crewmen got the assignment, and they were little more than spectators at a stunning fireworks display. In September, Van Kirk put in his papers, bade the others goodbye, and went home to Mary Jane. He was studying chemical engineering at Bucknell University when General Leslie Groves, who had run the Manhattan Project, passed through and tried to tempt him back into the service.

"I've had enough of *that* piece of cake," Van Kirk said.

Groves was a large, blustery man, accustomed to having his way. He was angry. Van Kirk didn't care.

He graduated from Bucknell into a job at Du Pont at twenty-nine, choosing it from among four or five offers, and never left. He started in a hard hat and goggles in a chemical plant in Niagara Falls, as a process engineer making four hundred dollars a month. But life on a factory floor didn't agree with him, and he applied for a transfer to the marketing side, which was what corporate America had begun calling sales. The professor who had pushed Van Kirk toward Du Pont wanted to know what the hell he had done *that* for; you didn't need brains for marketing, just a cast-iron stomach and a capacity for booze. Van Kirk had made up his mind. He was made to be a salesman; he had that winning smile, that radio-announcer voice, that aura of young self-confidence he had brought home with his medals from the war.

He lived his business life thereafter on the installment plan, moving from district office to district office as luck, opportunity, and the caprice of higher management required. He and his family learned to pull stakes quickly; once, Van Kirk built a brand-new house in Columbus, Georgia, and spent one night in it before moving on to the next stop.

He did two tours at company headquarters in Wilmington, trying to move from middle to higher management. It was not a want of application that stopped him; he gave himself to The Office—some people, he reckoned, might call him a workaholic—and for a time seemed well launched on a fast upward track. But he was not built for the politics of it, and each time he seemed to bump his head on an invisible ceiling. It beat being shot at, he thought, remembering the war. Still, he was happier in sales and in the less constricting life of the field offices, and he served out his days with Du Pont in a succession of proconsulates, in Columbus; Cincinnati; Los Angeles; Charlotte, North Carolina; and finally San Francisco.

The tract houses got bigger along the way; the family car multiplied to two and was joined at various posts by a power boat, a horse, and fleets of tricycles and bicycles to accommodate his growing brood. He and Mary Jane had four children, the first, Tom, and the last, Joanne, born nineteen years apart; their household might have been a permanent set for *Leave It To Beaver*. They had achieved a taste of the life, if not the leisure, of the upper middle class. And then one day in 1970, Mary Jane took ill. Her doctors said it was arteriosclerosis; Ted guessed later that it might have been Alzheimer's, a disease less understood then than now. Her memory and then her health ebbed away. In 1973, she died, and the comfortable little world of the Van Kirks fell apart.

Van Kirk did not realize how badly undone he was. He buried himself in his job and organized the family like an Army platoon to keep no more than a step behind the household chores. It wasn't working. He had been a widower for two unhappy years when a customer in Mobile invited him home for dinner and introduced him to Imogene Cumbie Guest, a receptionist, divorced, with two grown sons. He was fifty-four and Jean, as he came to call her, was fifty. He thought she was a gracious and attractive Southern lady. She thought he was one of the saddest-looking people she had ever seen. Even his clothes were a mess, and he didn't seem to give a damn about it; as it happened, he didn't *know* it. *God,* she told herself, *that's a man who needs help if I ever saw one.*

They started seeing each other—it was amazing how

much service Mobile got, Van Kirk thought afterward, for such a small amount of business—and, late that summer, they married. The pieces of Van Kirk's life came together. The children grew up, left home, found careers and mates, and began sending home snapshots of grandchildren—two of them by the summer of 1985. Joanne was last out of the nest, and Jean spoiled her ardently, having never had a daughter of her own. In 1978, Ted's last transfer took him to San Francisco; he occupied a handsome corner office in a ziggurat in Walnut Creek, running six sales reps, and settled in a four-bedroom, three-bath house on a golf course in Marin County.

At sixty-four, he had begun planning his retirement for the end of 1985. His hair, combed up in a single wave, was thinning and gray, and he wore bifocals, but time had otherwise been kind to him; he looked ten years younger than he was. He wore a faint air of regret at the roads not taken—at several lost chances to go into business for himself instead of indenturing himself for life to a single corporation. There had been one particularly inviting proposition, when he was in his early forties, to become a principal in a chemical-distributing company in the South. He had said no then and had regretted it later; if he were rewriting his life, he guessed, there were a lot of things he might change.

He had chosen what he saw as a pretty typical corporate existence instead, a nomad existence trying to move up by moving about. His children had all rejected that life-style for themselves, and he wondered in retrospect if he might not in fact have done better picking his spot somewhere and staying there. But Du Pont had rewarded him well for his gypsying, as he reminded himself whenever he sat beside his pool, or poured a fine California red from his own cellar, or played a round of hit-and-giggle golf with Jean and their friends. He did not, at such moments, envy those Silicon Valley yo-yos their entrepreneurial millions. Brooding was foreign to his disposition, anyway. The sunny side was almost always up for Van Kirk; if you counted the pluses instead of the minuses, he thought, life could look pretty darn good.

Neither did he rue the day his own life changed over Hiroshima. On the contrary, if the circumstances were the same, he thought, he would do the same thing again. He knew there had been controversy about the bomb almost from the day they dropped it. The 509th Composite Group had never been awarded so much as a Presidential Unit Citation, though they had arguably ended the war and were decorated individually for their service. It was as if the government was proud of the men of the *Enola Gay* singly and yet embarrassed by the mission that had brought them together.

The controversy seemed only to have begun with the end of the war. There were people who argued forty years after the fact that they hadn't needed to use the bomb at all—that Japan was licked by August 1945 and the destruction of Hiroshima and Nagasaki had been gratuitous acts of cruelty for no compelling military purpose. Van Kirk didn't believe it. He *couldn't* believe that the leaders of the nation had any other purpose in mind than the swift and successful prosecution of the war.

He, Tibbets, and Ferebee still saw one another, though rarely at reunions of the 509th. It was not shame that held them away; it was just that the unit was less a unit, really, than an assemblage, thrown together for what turned out to be two combat missions. Van Kirk and the others felt more at home among their older buddies from the European theater, people they really *knew*, reminiscing about their days together on the flying bucket of bolts they called *The Red Gremlin*.

That war had been a less complicated one, a black-and-white affair uncluttered by talk of sin and guilt. Tibbets particularly, as the skipper of the mission, had heard a lot of that talk and had tired of it; it was, he thought, as if there was a campaign out there to *make* him feel guilty and to demand that he justify what he had done. He felt no obligation to do so; it wasn't he who had attacked Pearl Harbor, the act which had started the war, and it wasn't he who had decided to bomb Hiroshima and Nagasaki, which had ended it. He had been a soldier in a war, and as Clausewitz said, the object of war was to impose your will on your enemy by whatever means were available to you.

The men of the *Enola Gay* found it unfortunate that, in the years following the war, the media had fixed on the gin-soaked maunderings of Claude Eatherly, the pilot of the weather plane that scouted Hiroshima, and made it look as if *all* of them were emotional basket cases. They weren't, not the men Van Kirk knew. Tibbets had made a success running a charter Learjet fleet in Ohio, Ferebee trading in real estate in Florida; their lives, like Van Kirk's own, were unscarred by the bomb. "Hell," Ferebee, who pushed the button, said as if for all of them, "it was a job. I did it."

It was a job, in Van Kirk's view, that had to be seen in the context of its time, as an act of war intended to end a war; taken in those terms, it had been an epic success, and they were heroes. There were still recriminations, still phone calls in the night from antibomb activists wanting the men of the *Enola Gay* to say they were sorry. They were not. When they journeyed afterward to Hiroshima and Nagasaki, they did not go, as Tibbets put it, to *regret* anything except the immutable fact that war is hell. Their consciences were clear, their minds untroubled. When a visitor asked Van Kirk if he had ever been bothered by guilt or bad dreams, he smiled and shook his head. He had come in off the mission, had a bite and a few beers, and hit the sack, and he had not lost a night's sleep over the bomb in forty years.

11

KAZ SUYEISHI PROWLED the conference room at City View Hospital in Los Angeles, reducing a Carlton to ash in quick, impatient puffs. "This mama-san is very pregnant," she said, holding out both hands as if to enfold a large imaginary belly, "but I don't know how many children I am going to have." Nine years before, on sheer brass, she had talked the government of Japan into sending over a team of doctors—experts in radiation problems—to examine *hibakusha* who had settled in America after the war. There were a lot of them, perhaps as many as a thousand around the country, but you had to *plead* with them to come out of hiding, belabor them for months in advance with ads and calls and begging letters, and you still wound up pacing the floor like a nervous parent waiting for the kids to come home. The doctors had been coming back every two years for eight years now, gradually widening their net, and Kaz still never knew how many survivors would show up. Forty years after the bomb, too many of them were still prisoners of their shame and their fear.

She knew their nightmares, because she had lived them herself in 1945 and dreamed them for many years afterward. It was as if the teenage girl named Kaz Tanaka had died the day she saw the bomb come floating down toward her like a scrap of paper against the sky; she had been granted a second life, and she thanked God for that, but it had been a *changed* life, plagued by ill health and bad dreams and, for too long, an abashed silence. That she had made something of it owed to her will, which was undamaged, and her wiry tensile strength. She moved to America, married happily, and, with some trepidation, had a child of her own; still, it was not until she broke the silence that the nightmares ended.

They had started in the ruins of her old life. Kaz's family had been luckier than most. Her father was in agony for weeks, lying outdoors on a tatami with his burns, and her brother's wounds refused to close. But they had at least survived, and they began, painfully, to rebuild their lives. They had two wells for water, and an ancient uncle who lived on an island off the coast brought them a great sack of food every week. Kaz's father found a carpenter willing to raise a new house out of the wreckage of the old, in exchange for whatever wood was left over. The house more nearly resembled a hovel, two slapsided rooms with not much more than tatami for furniture; Kaz could see the first snowflakes of winter through the cracks between the boards on the roof. By the standards of Hiroshima after the bomb, though, it was a mansion.

In time, the visible wounds healed. The burns on Kaz's father's chest left a tracery of ropy keloid scarring. He liked to say the scars made maps of Japan and America, side by side the way they ought to be, and when the subject of the bomb came up, he resisted blaming anyone. "The war," he would say, "is finished."

But as the others were recovering, Kaz had fallen ill with all the symptoms of radiation sickness. The malady was one of the frightening aftershocks of the bomb; the scientists in Los Alamos were surprised by its extent—

they had thought the *blast* would do most of the killing—and the doctors in Japan were unschooled in its treatment. All Kaz knew was that she felt as if she were dying. She was aflame with fever. She was nauseated and dizzy, almost as if she were drunk. Her gums and her bowels were bleeding. She looked like a ghost. A friend saw her one day, while she was still mobile, and did not recognize her; Kaz had to tell her, "Hi, it's me, it's me!"

By October, she had taken to her bed, her body ice-cold. She could barely breathe or eat; tangerines were the only food that tasted good to her, and as she grew weaker, she could not peel one without help, or even lift a single section to her lips. A doctor came to see her; he had heard of such cases, but had no idea what to do. "I can't save her," Kaz heard him saying through the haze of her illness. She found herself oddly unafraid. People were dying, she thought, dying every day; they would develop symptoms just like hers and then, one day, would disappear. *Well, I'm next,* she thought matter-of-factly; she was an eighteen-year-old girl waiting her turn to die.

In memory, she would mark the first day of 1946 as the start of her second life. It was an old superstition among the Japanese that a person would spend the entire year as he or she spent New Year's Day, and Kaz's mother was determined that Kaz would spend at least a bit of it on her feet. A neighbor helped; they wrapped Kaz in a kimono, got her outside, and propped her upright for a few wobbly minutes. The medicine worked better than anything in the doctor's kit bag, since the only known treatment for radiation sickness was rest. Kaz remained ill for a long time thereafter; it would be six months before she could stand alone. But death no longer seemed quite so inevitable, and as winter gave way to spring and spring to summer, she began to mend.

The illness had not really left her; it had gone into

hiding instead, and its aftereffects would trouble her all her life. But as she grew stronger, she felt a rekindled longing to see America. Her parents had other plans for her; her mother was training her in the traditional arts of cooking, sewing, and flower arranging, preparing her for marriage. It was 1949 when they relented, halfway, and sent her to Hawaii to study fashion. They expected she would soon get homesick and come back to them. She didn't; it would be years before they saw one another again.

Her two years in Hawaii began as a liberation from her memories, until the day a distinguished-looking Caucasian man planted himself in her path on a street in Honolulu. She tried to walk past him. He pointed a finger at her and blamed her for the American deaths at Pearl Harbor.

She was dumbfounded. "I'm an American, I'm an American," she protested. Her English was limited, and she felt it failing her. "Hiroshima, Hiroshima, bomb, bomb," she said, waving both arms toward the sky, and then, pointing at herself, "Hurt me! Hurt me!"

The man was staring at her.

"You're American," Kaz said, pointing at him. "I'm American. You, me—brother, sister. I don't hate you."

The man said nothing. She couldn't tell if she had made sense to him or not; she didn't know if he hated her or not.

The episode was like touching a match to a fuse. Kaz's nightmares came back, and so did her symptoms, the fevers and chills and a spooky purplish cast to her skin. She saw several doctors. None of them knew much about the toxic effects of neutrons and gamma rays on human beings 1.2 miles from the hypocenter of a nuclear explosion; no one did. They told her that her problems were psychological—that she was homesick and ought to go back to her mama and papa. She ignored them, and, when she was able, her sickness. She finished her classes and jollied her parents into sending her on to Pasadena, where she had been born. It was supposed to be a visit, a nostalgia trip, but Kaz stayed; she was home.

She was working as an apprentice in a dress factory when a young Nisei pattern-maker came in to see her boss. His name was Mas Suyeishi, and Kaz was immediately struck by his gentle ways and his smile; he reminded her of her father. With a girlfriend in tow, she visited his business and let him show her how the machinery worked. He asked her to dinner. She said yes. On their third date, he proposed, and she fainted.

Mas, as it turned out, had learned most of what he knew about the old Japanese ways from the movies; he was thoroughly American and had no idea that a man never popped the question directly to his love—he pressed his suit with her father, and then only through a matchmaker. His Americanization had persisted in spite of his own bitter experience of the war, some of it spent behind barbed wire in relocation centers—or, as he preferred, concentration camps. His parents had lived in America since the early years of the century, and Mas and his five brothers and sisters had been born there; his father was growing strawberries and raspberries on a parcel of leased land outside San Jose when the war began. The degree of their assimilation counted for nothing then against the fact of their ancestry. They were caught in the sweep-up of 120,000 Japanese-Americans and interned in the Wyoming outback as a threat to the security of the country. The sole evidence against them was their race.

Mas's faith in his country was strained by the experience; he would never be able to speak of it without a catch in his voice. His parents were broken by it. The whole family lived in a single room in a barracks and ate in a communal mess hall. Mas's father was assigned to Class A work status, the most menial, and found himself washing dishes at sixteen dollars a month. The job, in Japanese tradition, was considered women's work and therefore demeaning to a man. Mas's father endured it in silence, but the family could see his spirit crumble. When he was allowed to return to California after the war, he was too old to start his life over. Two of his daughters never married; it was his final defeat that they took jobs instead to support their parents.

Still, the parents endured, and Mas presented Kaz to them, once she had recovered from her swoon. They raised no obstacles to a marriage, not even when Kaz told them all about her experience of the bomb. Then she went to Hiroshima to see her own parents. It took a year merely to get them to address the question and two more for them to satisfy themselves, with the help of a private investigator, that Mas was worthy of their daughter's hand.

Partly as a result of the delay, the Suyeishis started late on their marriage, Mas at thirty-six and Kaz at thirty-one. Kaz wanted a baby right away; it would be her certification to herself that she was a woman like other women. The suspense began at conception—four different doctors told Kaz they could not promise her a normal baby—and her pregnancy was a difficult one. She gave birth to a daughter, Christiane, after much illness and more prayer. The first face she saw afterward was Mas's, looking grave.

"Is my baby—?" she began.

"Your baby is normal," Mas said. "Perfect."

The shadow of the cloud still lay over their lives. Kaz's sieges of illness persisted, and so did her nightmares; sometimes, she would dream of the bomb and pull the covers over Mas's head in her sleep, protecting him against the radiation. She tried to teach her daughter about the mark on her past without frightening her or making her feel different from other girls. They went to the Peace Memorial Museum in Hiroshima once, on a visit with Kaz's family, and Kaz was pleased that the word Chris found for her feelings was *kawaiso*—an expression not of fear for oneself but of sympathy for others who had suffered.

But anxiety lingered unspoken between them. Chris fainted at the zoo one suffocatingly hot day while she was still in junior high and had to lie down until she got her strength back.

"Is it something I might have inherited?" she asked Kaz when she got home.

"No, it's nothing unusual," Kaz said firmly. "Don't worry about it."

Kaz had grown accustomed by then to keeping her fears to herself. She did not surrender to them, or to her illnesses; she repressed them instead and found refuge learning arts and crafts, attending class any day she felt well enough to walk. When a friend invited her to a meeting of American *hibakusha*, her first response was no thanks. She was trying to *forget* her past, not relive it. She didn't want to get involved.

But she allowed herself to be tempted to a subsequent meeting and was present at the birth of the Committee of Atomic Bomb Survivors in the United States, a cause that came to occupy the center of her life. She was frightened at first, merely talking about the day of the bomb and the days after; she had been like the other *hibakusha*, hiding their stigmata even from their families, and she had to push herself to speak. What she discovered in the committee was that she was not alone—that there were others who had seen what she had seen and endured what she had endured. It began to seem almost a holy calling to speak and act, an obligation to God for having brought her back from the dead, and she flung herself into it. The family deferred to her obsession. Mas chauffeured her to her endless meetings. The housework suffered. The bad dreams stopped.

Kaz's personal cause was the medical problems of survivors; at fifty-eight, she was herself a walking catalogue of them. Cataracts were forming in both eyes—"my

Cadillacs," she called them. Her gums had given out; it finally became simpler to have all her teeth removed and use dentures instead. She had passages of weakness from the radiation and chronic back problems from her injuries. She chose her clothing carefully, favoring pants or skirts long enough to cover the scars on her legs.

She had felt not only the pain of the *hibakusha* but their powerlessness as well—the uninterest of Washington in their problems and the unwillingness of medical insurers to cover their special claims. It occurred to her that if America wouldn't help, Japan might. She was planning a trip to see her family in 1976; before she left, she wrote a reporter she had known, remarking that she would like to get a message on the problems of the American *hibakusha* to the right person in the Japanese government.

The friend took her literally at her word. She deplaned at Tokyo into a blaze of flashbulbs and a surge of reporters asking for copies of her message.

"*What* message?" she asked. She hadn't brought one, not in writing; it was all in her heart.

She was still groping for the right words when the Minister of Welfare, Masami Tanaka, received her in his offices. But he seemed a kindly man, not at all forbidding; *he will rescue me,* Kaz thought, and she recovered her speech. She told him about the travail of the American survivors, physical and financial, and about her dream of having a doctor come see them—a *Japanese* doctor who spoke their language and understood their problems. "The United States is our country, our father," she said. "But the children have a problem, and for some reason the father cannot help. Japan is the mother. I came back to ask my mother, 'Please help. Please don't let us down.' "

They met twice more, and the next year, the doctors began coming, not one but a team offering examinations and counsel free of charge. People were hesitant at first, as if, one of the doctors thought, they were still hostage to the bomb after thirty years. They had lived too long with their fear of the unknown—an angst so deep that, if they got the sniffles, they thought they were going to die.

Having someone Japanese to confide in helped, as Kaz had supposed; the itinerary grew from one city to four by 1983, and the team saw 305 survivors, perhaps a third of the American *hibakusha*. The program was plainly successful, and a fifth city was added to the tour in 1985. But the fear remained a powerful adversary, and Kaz, preparing for the visitation, had begun her drumming four months in advance of the doctors.

You never knew how it would come out, she thought, pacing the hospital floor in an aureole of Carlton smoke. You wrote letters and placed ads and put promos on TV and took people to lunch; you begged and scolded and nagged like a mama-san, and you still didn't know if they would all show up. A woman from Kentucky, a GI bride named Kay Mitchell, had become a special cause to her, a four-month project. Mrs. Mitchell had been a schoolgirl of fourteen, riding a streetcar across a bridge, when the bomb fell; she had been blown into the river, badly cut, and when she had made her way home, she had found her mother dying of burns.

She had been living in the States for nearly thirty years, but she had only just heard about the doctors and had called Kaz for the information. Kaz had written her three times. She hadn't answered, not one word, and Kaz was as worried as if it were her own daughter. "She should *be* here." Kaz told herself. "She might not come."

Others were arriving, and Kaz was counting heads like a producer on opening night. Some were people she knew from past years. "S'ishi-san, S'ishi-san!" they called, seeing her, and when she embraced them, tears flooded her eyes. Others were first-timers, people who had been afraid to come before. "You're just like a groundhog," she chided one of them, a shy man in his fifties whose vision had been failing. "How come you're hiding like this?" Soon, she had him laughing.

A woman materialized, another of Kaz's projects. She had phoned in great distress, frightened in equal measure about her health and having her secret known; she had never even told her husband she was a *hibakusha*. "You come, and I will protect you," Kaz had told her. "I'm Kaz and I will protect you one hundred percent." She came.

So, at last, did Mrs. Mitchell. Kaz looked up and there she was, standing with Mas in the doorway, a short, trim woman in a black-and-beige checked dress.

"Kay Mitchell from Kentucky?" Kaz asked.

Mas nodded.

"She's here, she's here!" Kaz cried, as excited as a schoolgirl at Christmas; she was jumping up and down and clapping her hands and telling everyone it was Kay-san, all the way from Kentucky. "It's me, Kaz!" she said, pointing at her name on a sticker on her dress. "I'm the one who sent you all those letters. Why didn't you answer?"

Mrs. Mitchell made her apologies. She had been embarrassed to answer, she said; Kaz's letters were so beautiful, and her own Japanese had grown so rusty with disuse.

"But you're *here*!" Kaz exclaimed.

The headcount had been going well; the doctors would see 106 people in four days in Los Angeles alone, 20 more than in 1983, and would examine 340 in all on their five-city itinerary. But Kaz had a painterly eye, and it was Kay-san from Kentucky who somehow finished the picture for her. She had come, and seen the doctors, and been pronounced fine, and Kaz's pleasure was complete. *This mama-san had a lot of children,* she was thinking, her face aglow. *I'm so glad I had so many.*

12

NOT ALL THE *hibakusha* were as lucky as Kaz, or as gifted at the arts of survival. Fortune had spared Yoshio Kanazawa's life alone among the six children in his family, but he paid a kind of double indemnity for it. As a *hibakusha,* he was left alone and in chancy health; as the child of Korean immigrants, he was the victim of old and virulent ethnic prejudices that stirred to renewed life after the war. The combined weight of his burdens stunted his future. He grew up unschooled and unlettered; forty years after the bomb, he lived in a modest city-subsidized apartment in Hiroshima's Korean ghetto and was trapped by his illiteracy in a dead-end job.

Sachiko Ota's life, too, was in some measure victim to the *pika-doun.* She had been four months pregnant when the second atomic bomb leveled nearly half of Nagasaki and buried her in the rubble of her boarding house. She and her husband escaped with their lives, but she fell seriously ill with radiation sickness. Her gums were bleeding, her teeth were loose, her hair was coming out, her stomach stopped growing, and her body was covered with tiny violet spots hardly bigger than pinpricks. Nobody knew what the spots meant, not then, but they were feared among the *hibakusha;* people with no outward sign of injury would suddenly develop them and, soon after, would die.

Sachiko survived, but she was frightened for her unborn child, and when she gave birth to a son, Masanobu, in January 1946, her fears were realized. His head was abnormally small—the word the doctors used was microcephalic—and he was severely retarded. He could not care for himself, and for many years, the government would not help. Masanobu was in his twenties before the bureaucracy formally classified him a *hibakusha* and thus eligible for aid. He was granted a stipend then, and was placed part-time in a government-supported workshop in the reconstructed city, making shopping bags.

The Otas were modest and accepting people; they counted themselves blessed that three younger sons had been born healthy and had got their college diplomas. They bore the burden of Masanobu's care with love and without complaint, not even against the people who had dropped the bomb. Sachiko's husband, Shigetoshi, had been in the military himself for five and a half years; he understood that the destruction of Nagasaki had been an act of war. It couldn't be helped, and if his eldest son had paid a terrible price, there was consolation in his very simplicity; it could at least be said that there were no sins on Masanobu Ota's soul.

For some of the *hibakusha,* there was no consolation at all, no exit from suffering except death. Yoko Sasaki was almost one of them. That she had survived her burns at all was an act of sheer will, a cry of defiance against the doctor who had drawn a cloth over her face and pronounced her all but dead. She had clung to existence, and during a long, slow convalescence at her grandparents' home in the country, the burns on her face and forearms healed and hardened into thick, fibrous keloid scars. She was left then with her inner pain, and her convalescence from it took most of a lifetime.

Her disfigurement fell like a veil between her and the

world. Children teased her in the village streets, and her grandfather, a teacher of the tea ceremony, required that she stay out of sight when his pupils came for their lessons; he did not want her embarrassing them with the mark of the bomb. When she could not bear the taunts and stares, she would go off walking in the hills by herself. There was a special place she loved, a private place on an emerald-green ridge where she would sit with her brushes and ink and practice her Chinese calligraphy; there, in her solitude, she could lose herself in her brush strokes and in the natural beauty of her surroundings.

For a time, she found a second haven in school. Her teachers were kind, and her classmates at least polite, if not precisely friendly; she rose quickly to the top of her class, and it became possible for her to feel like a normal girl again. But the world kept instructing her that she was not. She wanted to be in the school play. Her teachers excluded her, without saying why; she could only suppose that it was because of her scars. Her deliverer was a young English teacher who organized his own play around her, casting Yoko in the only female role. He was handsome and gentle, and Yoko developed a schoolgirl crush on him. He was her first love, and the new emotions stirring within her made the ruin of her features even harder to bear.

She was entering that age when friends and relations were pairing off and getting married; even her younger sister found a match, though it was Yoko's prerogative as the elder to marry first. She sat through the weddings in a torment of envy and rage, but when she spoke of her own longings, her mother told her bluntly, "You've got keloid scars all over your face. Forget about marriage, and stay at home with me." Yoko suppressed her feelings, resisting her mother's counsel and yet suspecting it was so. *Who,* she thought, *would want someone like me?*

She was twenty-five and past the usual marrying age when a suitor magically appeared, a presentable enough young man who seemed to see the beauty beneath her scar tissue. Yoko's mother refused to see him, and her brother-in-law tried to discourage the relationship; it was well known in Hiroshima that there were men who would marry women with burn scars for money or the kind regard of the community. Yoko, in her desperation, wouldn't listen, and she and her young man were married.

Her disillusion was swift and brutal. She and her husband moved in with his parents, in a threadbare household in a neighboring town. They had barely arrived when her new in-laws began demanding to know why she hadn't brought a dowry. Her husband, as it turned out, had no steady work and soon stopped looking even for day jobs. He spent what money there was on alcohol; when their son, Ayumu, was born, she had to pawn her sewing machine to buy milk. Her husband beat her with his fists and, more cruelly, with words; with a scarface like hers, he said, she ought to pay him for having married her at all.

She fled to a tiny apartment in Hiroshima, paying the deposit with borrowed money. He rarely visited, and when he did, he beat her all over again. She finally could endure no more; one New Year's Day, she took a whole bottle of sleeping pills and, with little Ayumu beside her, lay down to die. The attempt was a last essay in futility. She wakened with her son tugging at her sleeve; he hadn't eaten since she had gone to sleep, and he was hungry. The city was caught up in its holiday revels. Yoko had been unconscious for three days, and no one had even noticed that she was missing.

She took hold of her life after that and tried again, alone with her son in a tiny flat of the sort the Japanese refer to self-deprecatingly as a rabbit hutch. She never saw her husband after 1966; in 1970, they were divorced. What hopes remained to her, in her fifties, were invested vicariously in her son. Her own future had withered and died in the white light of the bomb.

13

FOR OTHERS of the *hibakusha,* hope somehow survived, a life force as stubborn and resilient as a flower growing through the cracks in a city sidewalk. The bomb had turned Mary Fujita's husband to ash, all of him except his handsome white teeth, and she and her son, Gene, had both been sickened by radiation. Both recovered and repatriated to their second home, America, in the years after the war; Gene went into real estate, and Mary opened a beauty shop in Seattle. In her middle seventies, her health problems suddenly reappeared: a low white-blood-cell count and a run of mysterious infections. But she was still doing hair for residents of a nursing home near her bungalow on the edge of town, and she was untroubled by her symptoms. If a doctor told her she were going to die tomorrow, she thought, she would not be afraid. That she had endured as long and as hardily as she had seemed magical to her, a wondrous gift; she had outlived the Hiroshima she remembered and a hundred thousand of its inhabitants by forty years.

A kindred spirit dwelled in Yasuko Yamaguchi, though she had been orphaned at twelve by the bomb and had watched her sister die soon after in an agony of illness and guilt. She got by alone in the impoverished world of postwar Japan, paying her own way with a series of odd jobs; at various times, she waited on tables, made baskets for tangerines, and worked as a scribe at City Hall. She managed somehow to continue her schooling, with distinction enough to qualify her for a scholarship at Hiroshima University.

She was still, in her fifties, a petite and attractive woman; there were traces of sadness in her eyes and of loss in her smile, but when she spoke of her life, it was as if she were describing a victory in battle. She had married a fellow *hibakusha,* raised four children, and still carried on her career, teaching the blind. She thought often of the family she had lost and particularly of her sister Hatsuko, forcing herself to live long enough to tell Yasuko that the others were dead. Their legacy to Yasuko was her own fierce independence; if she had had anyone left to lean on, she imagined long afterward, she might not have made it at all.

Shigeko Sasamori made it because she *did* have someone to lean on; it was, she liked to say, as if she had been blessed in life with three fathers. The first was the man she had been born to; he and her mother had found her in a school auditorium, burned beyond recognition, and had nursed her back to life. The second was a Methodist pastor named Kiyoshi Tanimoto, a small, eloquent man with Old Testament eyes and a calling to serve young women who, like Shigeko, had been disfigured by the bomb. Her life, till their paths crossed, had been lived in a kind of half-light; her face and hands were thickly scarred, and she passed most of her days at home, sheltered against the taunts and the pity of the world.

But she chanced one day to walk past Tanimoto's church and heard singing from within. Something drew her inside, though she had been raised a Buddhist, and once inside, she knew she had found a second home, a place where her scars seemed to matter less than her possibilities. Tanimoto had gathered a group of burn victims—the Society of Keloid Girls, they were called then—and had organized a center for their rehabilitation. There were Bible classes, and instruction in sewing, and for twenty-five of the luckiest, some Society members and some from the outside, the prospect of a trip to America for corrective surgery. Shigeko was one of them.

They were dubbed the Hiroshima Maidens, and while they encountered some resentment in Japan for seeking treatment in the land of the enemy, their journey attracted the interest and the sympathy of the world. Their sponsor in the States was Norman Cousins, then editor of *Saturday Review;* he organized the flights and the treatment programs and stood as a kind of paterfamilias to all the Maidens. But Shigeko was special to him, a part of his own family. She settled in the United States, in important part because he was there; she thought of him as her third father, and her last.

She had begun her course of surgery in Japan, and continued it at Mount Sinai Hospital in New York; there were thirty operations in all. She made a good candidate, partly by the sheerest chance. For reasons she had long forgotten, she had worn two pairs of pants the day of the bomb. The outer pair burned off; only the waistband was left when her mother undressed her. But the inner pair protected her lower body, and there was plenty of healthy skin for grafts.

The surgery, as for most of the Maidens, could not completely undo what the bomb had done. Thirty years later, Shigeko's lower face and arms were still scarred, and her fingers were twisted and misshapen. But something in her manner, in the absence of self-consciousness or self-pity, made people forget what was blemished about her; they remembered her soft, black hair and her large, expressive eyes instead, and thought of her as almost beautiful.

She had wanted to be a nurse but could not because of her hands. Still, she was able to work in kindred jobs in hospitals and elsewhere, usually caring for babies, and she had a son of her own in a brief marriage to a Japanese student; she named the infant Norman Cousins Sasamori. She did not hide her past from him, as so many of the *hibakusha* hid it from their families; she spoke openly about it and made it a part of his inheritance. To be silent did not occur to her. People forgot too easily, she thought; if they were not reminded of the past, they would repeat it. It was her duty to speak, her *mission.* She could imagine no other reason why God had allowed her to survive.

14

It was one thing for the *hibakusha* to speak and another to be heard across the great distance between the conqueror and the conquered, the warriors and the casualties of war. It was no longer ill will that separated them but lapsed time. The *hibakusha* had become artifacts of a past the world preferred, on the whole, to forget; they were history, and when they intruded on the present, they were disturbers of the peace.

Kaz Suyeishi tried, in the summer of 1985. It was the season of remembrances, and her story had appeared in *Newsweek,* along with Ted Van Kirk's; they had attracted the notice of the *Today* show, and its producers invited Kaz, Van Kirk, and Tom Ferebee, the bombardier, to appear on the eve of the anniversary of the destruction of Hiroshima.

There was a great deal Kaz wanted to say, a "powerful message" on behalf of all the *hibakusha;* she could barely sleep the night before the show, trying to sort the thoughts tumbling in her mind. She wanted to reach out to the fliers in friendship. She wanted to talk about how her own life had ended in 1945, and how she had been granted a second life of forty years to speak out against war and suffering. She wanted to say that the peace of the world over that time had been just an *imitation* peace, an interval in which no bombs happened to have fallen. She wanted to talk about the need for a *real* peace, a hundred percent guaranteed peace; destroy all the bombs, she wanted to say, and all the world's people would be good friends, because the cause of their unease would be gone.

It didn't work out. There was too little time—the hard news of the day had impinged on the ten and a half minutes blocked out for remembering the bomb—and too much artifice in the confrontation. Peter Ueberroth, the commissioner of baseball, was in the green room waiting to go on when Kaz arrived; they were joined by Pat Boone, the singer, tan of skin and gold of chain, and Tom Seaver, the pitcher, who had just won his three-hundredth game. Kaz surmised that the two middle-aged gentlemen sitting across the room from her were Van Kirk and Ferebee, but no one introduced them, and they did not speak. Their meeting had been contrived to fill a few minutes of air time between Ueberroth on an impending baseball players' strike and Boone on Christian rock videos; they were part of the day's disposable batch of newsmakers, the morning shift on the network wake-up shows.

Soon, nine of them filled the room, at close quarters and with little common ground. Kaz asked Boone for his autograph.

"It will make my daughter very happy," she said.

Boone looked flattered. He signed his name for her.

Ferebee, large and ruddy, was called away to be made up.

"He needs it more than I do," Van Kirk teased.

In a few minutes, Ferebee was back, freshly powdered.

"He doesn't look a bit better," Van Kirk said, smiling.

There was not much more to say. The people in the room were mostly staring in silence at the green-room monitor, watching the baseball segment, when Kaz was called into the studio. Baseball gave way to a grainy sequence of the *Enola Gay* taking off from Tinian on its Hiroshima run.

Van Kirk glanced at it. His face was expressionless. When pictures of the drop came on, the mushroom cloud rising skyward and spreading across the screen, he was looking the other way.

The scene shifted to a contemporary shot of Peace Memorial Park, at the center of the reconstructed city.

"You ever been there, Pat?" Seaver called across the room. He was signing baseballs for the *Today* staff.

"Yes," Boone answered. "It's incredible, isn't it?"

"Absolutely unbelievable," Seaver agreed.

Kaz was on the screen, and her solo turn was not going very well. It had been compressed to two and a half minutes, far too little time for all she wanted to say; she was answering questions in monosyllables, almost as if she were husbanding what seconds there were for her message of peace and goodwill.

Had she seen the bomb fall?

"Oh, yes."

Had she been terrified?

"No. To me, B-29 was a silver-colored angel. . . . They never hurted anything."

Did she remember what happened when it went off?

"No. Unconscious."

Had she been hurt?

"Yes."

Seriously?

"Yes."

Radiation sickness, perhaps?

She had her opening at last, an opportunity to say something about the medical needs of the American *hibakusha*, but she had barely begun when her time ran out.

Van Kirk and Ferebee had been brought onto the set, and Kaz, changing seats during a break, crossed in front of them. No one introduced them, so she did it herself, grabbing their hands and announcing, "I'm Kaz." They smiled at her. They *couldn't* be angry with her, she thought; she had made herself their friend.

Their time on camera together was no less awkward for her gesture. Bryant Gumbel, conducting the interview, asked the men if they felt uncomfortable with Kaz. "No, no," they replied, nearly in unison, "not at all." Moments later, he asked Kaz if she bore any personal feelings toward them and she said, "No, none at all." But there was little connection between them. Kaz's conscious life centered around her experience of the bomb. Van Kirk and Ferebee had as consciously put it behind them, burying the memory with their other souvenirs of the war.

"I've talked more about the bomb in the last two weeks than I have in the last forty years," Van Kirk said.

"Does that bother you?" Gumbel asked.

"Talking about it?" Van Kirk replied. "No."

"When somebody brings it up, that's the one time I think about it," Ferebee said. "It was just another flight to me."

When Kaz spoke of her trauma, the inner scars that never disappear, Van Kirk smiled gently, almost tenderly, and Ferebee said he felt sorry for the people on the ground who had been killed or injured. "But we were sent there to do a job, to help end the war," he said, "so I can't say I'm sorry I did the mission. . . . Many millions had been killed before that."

"You were just doing a job," Gumbel said.

"That's the way I look at it," Ferebee answered.

"I know there's been a lot of argument about this," Van Kirk cut in. Something heavy, almost weary, in his tone suggested he had been over the same ground many times before. "But I still believe that anybody who looks at the facts that were available at that time can only conclude that dropping the bomb was the proper thing to do to bring the bloodiest war that we've ever seen to a quick and, from our point of view, successful conclusion."

The camera found Kaz. She was nodding in agreement with the two fliers or, more accurately, sympathy for their situation. They had been military men, she thought, soldiers following orders in a war. She didn't hate them. She *couldn't*. They hadn't meant to hurt her. They had had no choice.

"In my personal opinion," Van Kirk was saying, "the people that say that many lives were saved because there was not an invasion of Japan—I'm talking here about both Japanese and American and other people's lives—I think that that conclusion is a proper one."

Kaz wanted to *say* what she felt for the two fliers, that they were like brothers to her, but the time was gone. The segment ended. She crossed over to Van Kirk and Ferebee again.

"We need to help each other, that's what I think," she said. She told Van Kirk she would like to get together with him sometime and asked what part of California he was from.

Near San Francisco, Van Kirk said. He was in the book; she could look him up.

Kaz retreated to the green room and, just to be sure, got his number from a *Today* operative. "They're nice gentlemen," she said, snuffling. "We'll get together."

Tears filled her eyes. Boone saw her distress. "You did terrific," he said.

Kaz wasn't so sure. The time had been too short for her to get her message out. She wanted to talk to Van Kirk, she said. She *needed* him; they had both experienced the first atomic bomb, and they should be working together to stop the next war. They should be friends.

She was thinking about that, leaving the studio, and about the things she hadn't had time to say in her precious few minutes speaking to the world. "I hate war!" she said to herself once, and then again. She was crying.

15

FOR MANY YEARS, Larry Johnston had imagined that he, too, would someday meet a victim of the bomb. He had often encountered Japanese professors in his work, and had always found occasion to explain how and why he had helped make the world's first atomic weapons. They had unfailingly replied that they understood, that there had after all been a war on; some even dared suggest that Japan had brought the devastation on itself by its aggression. But none of them had actually experienced the bombings, or suffered personal loss because of them, and their sympathy, while welcome, was not wholly satisfying. Johnston wanted something more than understanding, something only a person who had been maimed or had lost a loved one could give him. If a barrier lingered between them, he wanted it to fall.

He was not driven by guilt, as some of his more emotive colleagues seemed to him to be. He was impatient with their handwringing and with their talk of having struck a Faustian bargain with the devil, trading their souls for the terrible secrets of the bomb. He did not feel he had wronged anyone by his participation; on the contrary, he and his fellow scientists had helped liquidate the first global war with their invention, and so had nothing to feel guilty about. Yet Johnston accepted that people had been injured as a consequence of his labors, however honorable his intentions. He imagined that if he had been a GI and had killed a man face to face in battle, he might seek out the widow to ask absolution. Only someone who had suffered by his work could offer him that, and for years he imagined such a meeting, rehearsing in his mind what he would say.

The opportunity came one night in 1984 at a potluck supper at the student union at the University of Idaho, where Johnston had found his niche at mid-career. The occasion was the Chinese New Year, and the victim, unexpectedly, was Chinese, an agronomist named Chia-Tsang Liu; his brother had been a medical student in Hiroshima, and had been killed by the bomb. An acquaintance, hearing of Johnston's quest, pointed him out across the room, and Johnston made his way through the crowd to meet him. He introduced himself and once again, in meticulously chosen words, explained his part in the making of the bomb. Then, as he had always planned, he asked forgiveness for it.

"I know you didn't realize you might be killing some Chinese," the professor said, being gracious.

"Thank you," Johnston said. "And do you *forgive* me?"

The answer, as he had dared hope, was yes.

Johnston had come home in the late summer of 1945, bronzed by the Tinian sun, and had made for Berkeley to resume his graduate studies. He had detoured only briefly to Los Alamos, long enough for hellos and goodbyes. Some of his colleagues would return to the mesa to build the hydrogen bomb, a monster a thousand times more destructive than the rude firecracker they had dropped on Hiroshima; at its first test in the Pacific in 1952, an *island* would disappear. A second nuclear arms race was beginning, against Stalin this time instead of

Hitler, and Los Alamos would soon tingle with the old life and the old urgency again.

Johnston was never tempted. He did not question Harry Truman's decision to go on from the atomic to the thermonuclear age. If the president had asked *his* advice, he would in fact have urged that the quest for the H-bomb go forward; the "super," as they had called it in Los Alamos when it was still just a gleam in Edward Teller's eye, was going to be invented, and it seemed to Johnston vastly preferable that the Americans, not the Russians, have it first. Still, he would always have mixed feelings about bombs numerous and powerful enough to blow away not just a city but a continent, and having done his service in the war, he was anxious in any case to get on with his life and his work.

His patron, Luis Alvarez, abhorred empty time; he had used the flight home from Tinian to talk to Johnston about the particle accelerator they were going to build once they were back in the States, and when they had resettled in Berkeley, they did. The work paid for the family's groceries, and for Johnston's Ph.D. He did tours thereafter at Minnesota and Stanford universities and at an Air Force laboratory in Los Angeles, doing basic as against applied science. He built two more accelerators; he studied infrared light; he made a name in his profession for his work on the behavior of protons. But he began to feel, in the middle 1960's, that he wasn't making the contribution he ought to be making—that his theoretical physics might have suffered from his years in the laboratory. He wanted to get back to teaching, and in 1967 he settled with Millie and their five children in the sculptured green hills of northern Idaho.

He never left or cared to. He was no longer at one of the great wellheads of physical science, as he had been at Berkeley, say, or Los Alamos during the war, but that seemed a tolerable price for his contentment. He lived surrounded by God's beauty, wilderness lands and waters where he and Millie could camp and canoe, and presided over a wondrously cluttered laboratory of his own. He did his best thinking there, in the scent of oil vapors and the soft thump of a vacuum pump; a twelve-foot laser he had made himself stood haloed in a pinkish glow.

The work he and his students were pursuing, in far-infrared light, was unlikely to alter the course of human history as the Manhattan Project had; still, it opened new and challenging points of entry into the study of molecules. His personal life was comfortable, his professional life rewarding. His only souvenirs of the war were a ragged army-issue shirt—he still put it on when Millie cut his hair—and a hen-tracked dollar bill marked "Hiroshima Express." It was one of the pleasures of his autumn years that people rarely bothered him about the bomb anymore.

That had not always been so. It pained him that he could not have a civil conversation with his own daughter Ginger about war or nuclear weapons. She had grown up to be an evangelical missionary carrying the gospel to the Third World, which pleased Johnston greatly. But she had come of political age at the Berkeley of the sixties, a place grown as foreign to him as another country; he and his daughter seemed to him incapable of being rational on certain questions, and so tried to avoid them.

Johnston was upset as well by the coolness he had encountered among some of his fellow scientists, a palpable chill of disapproval for his work on the bomb. Berkeley hadn't been so bad, given the number of Manhattan Project alumni who had settled there; when they talked nuclear politics, their common ground was the danger of the future, not remorse for the past. But Johnston had felt a kind of disapprobation among perhaps a third of his colleagues on the physics faculty at Minnesota during his time there, and from some of his peers at

Idaho as well. Idaho was a conservative campus, and he was a popular teacher; the students were rarely rude to him on that subject, or any other. But the faculty was not always so restrained. One colleague could barely bring himself to speak to Johnston; his silence was like a wall between them until Johnston cornered him one day and set forth his complex thoughts on the bomb and the war.

Not everybody was willing to hear him out. The bomb had polarized physics as it had the larger American society in the years after the war; it was an emotional subject, and minds once made up were not easily shaken free of their conviction. Johnston was not a political animal in any case. Some of the great figures of the Manhattan Project, the Fermis and the Bethes, became crusaders for international control of atomic weapons. Johnston had done some speeches, too, in the early years, but he saw no realistic possibility of a new world order and therefore no practical sense in advocating it. His message instead was that Pandora's box, now open, could not be closed. Any country with the will, the time, and the money could build its own bomb; the only way to make the world safe was to change the hearts of humankind.

But with time, Johnston disengaged from the politics of the bomb. He found a kind of futility in arguing and rearguing the decisions of 1945, as if he were speaking in an echo chamber. Some of his colleagues seemed to him almost *smug* in their certitude that he had been wrong; it was as if they wanted him to repent so they could welcome him, a sinner redeemed, to the society of righteous men. There were days when they tried his patience and he dismissed them in his mind as a bunch of peaceniks. Mostly, he tried to remember that he was a man of science, obliged by calling to keep an open mind. He wished some of his antagonists would do the same. It was hard finding a decent argument on the bomb; he was willing to defend his views, and to entertain the case that he might have been wrong, but people seemed not to want to listen.

What he wanted to say was that he was not one of the handwringers, the men like Oppie who went to their graves weighted down by guilt at having placed all mankind at risk. They were, in his view, second-guessing honest decisions taken by reasonable men for good cause in the vortex of a world war. It was true, he agreed, that the planet had become unsafe with the dawning of the atomic age in Los Alamos and Hiroshima. But the bomb could not have been stopped from happening then any more than it could be disinvented now; it was an idea whose time had come.

It was likewise true that the contrivance they called the Gadget had caused great pain. It was characteristically American, in Johnston's view, to believe that no one should inflict suffering in any circumstance. He thought about the people who had been killed and injured, and was not without regret at what they had endured; they were God's children, too. But he did not wake up in the night tormented by their ghosts. In the insanity that was war, suffering became a relative thing, not an absolute. It was Oppie himself who had driven them on, reminding them constantly that the bomb was a means to the end of an awful worldwide conflagration. They had caused suffering to end suffering, and had saved hundreds of thousands of lives.

Johnston felt himself answerable in any case to higher authority than the peace people and the revisionist historians presuming to judge him and his colleagues from the safe distance of time. He remained a devout Christian, as he had always been, and his faith had to assimilate the fact of the bomb and his part in its manufacture. Fortune had made him the only person on the planet to have witnessed each of the three explosions that had heralded the coming of the nuclear age: the test in New Mexico and bombings of Hiroshima and Nagasaki. In the years after the war, he had sat through sermon after sermon likening the experiment on the Jornada del Muerto in July 1945 to the biblical prophecies of the end of the world—previsions of the sky peeling back like a scroll and of fire and blood raining down on the earth. He was too much the scientist, too precise in his habits of thought, to accept the analogy at face value. He *knew* what was happening when the Gadget went off, and why; the behavior of atoms under bombardment was obedient to physical law.

But Johnston was open to the possibility that something final might in fact have begun that day in the New Mexico desert—that the countdown toward the return of the Lord to earth might have been pushed up a notch or two. He believed in any case that there would be a Last Judgment, whether or not in the form so vividly anticipated in the Book of Revelation. Satan would be there as his accuser, arguing for his damnation, and his involvement with the bomb might be one of the charges dredged up against him; maybe, he thought, it was quite literally a hell of a thing he had done.

But Larry Johnston felt no less confident of his own salvation. He had spent his years trying to do right and had regularly sought God's help in discerning what it was; he had placed his own life in God's hands, and that would be decisive. He knew on faith that he would not be alone at the judgment seat. Let Satan accuse him of murder, he thought; in the remote event that he *was* judged wrong, Jesus would still be there beside him, saying, "Well, yes, that *was* a hell of a thing, but here—I've paid the price. He's one of mine," Jesus would say. "That one's on me."

16

"Let's assume, young lady," Billy Bryan Burns was saying. "that neither one of us had the atomic bomb, and let's assume that the Russians have twice as many human beings as we do, and the Chinese have three or four times the amount of human beings we do. What is the deterrent to war? How do we defend ourselves? Do we negotiate from weakness?" He smiled broadly, a father-knows-best kind of smile. "Without the bomb, I think we would be in a terrible, terrible position," he went on. "If we can keep from making a mistake, I think it's the greatest thing we've ever had in the whole world."

"But where are we heading, *Daddy?" his little girl Dottie answered. She was Dorothy Burns Douglas now, forty-six, married and the mother of two, but she was still his little girl.*

"We're not going anywhere, Dottie honey," Billy said. "We're going to stay static, honey, in this position of no war, until hopefully the U.S. finds some way to neutralize communism."

They sat over lunch at a handsome country club in North Carolina one noonday in the summer of 1985, talking seriously about the bomb for practically the first time since Dorothy was in high school. It wasn't a family subject, in Billy's eyes; he reckoned he and his own wife hadn't spent more than four hours talking about it, total, since the day he came home by liberty ship from Tinian in 1945. Other people were paid to worry about nuclear weapons, knowledgable people in the White House and the Pentagon. Billy didn't give the subject much of his time. He didn't feel he had to.

He had been in an expansive mood, seating his daughter and a guest at his table. His white Eldorado was out on the lot, and his navy blazer, his Kelly green pants, and his golf-course tan fairly radiated money and ease. He moved about the club with the assurance of a man who owned the place, as, fractionally, he did; he and Helen Burns were building their dream home on the grounds for his retirement. But a luncheon of fruit salad and iced coffee languished half-forgotten between father and daughter in the intensity of their family quarrel. They had become *America* debating across the divide between the generations and the sexes, talking about how much longer the world would or could survive the bomb.

Forever was Billy Bryan Burns's guess, when he dwelled on the matter at all. Mostly, if he could avoid it, he did not. He had loaded the first primitive A-bombs, waved them off for Hiroshima and Nagasaki, and thought little more about them at the time than that they were his ticket home; case closed. He reckoned long afterward that he might have gone crazy if he had *seen* the mushroom clouds, but he hadn't, and if he had had nightmares about the war on his return, as his wife and daughter said he had, he did not remember them. Sometimes he wondered why he *didn't* feel guilty about what the bomb had done. Sometimes he thought he should feel guilty for not feeling guilty.

He had had other things on his mind in the years after the war; he had been too busy seeking his fortune, and to his way of thinking, the bomb had made the world safe for him and people like him to do so. His generation had come back feeling good about the country and themselves, and had created more wealth, raised more houses, fathered more babies, and realized the American dream more times over than any in our history. Billy still felt a tingle just thinking about all the men he knew —guys he had grown up with in south Florida—who had got rich after the war. Sometimes, it brought tears to his eyes.

Billy Burns was one of them, a millionaire at sixty-six. He had started with a seven-thousand-dollar nest egg and a correspondence-school certificate in general insurance, and had pyramided them into a fortune in insurance, real estate, and mortgage lending. He had had a sideline in elective politics as commissioner of the Port of Palm Beach for twenty-two years and was talked about for governor of Florida. But turning money into more money was his gift and his calling. A savings and loan he started in West Palm Beach with some partners was the fastest growing in the nation when a larger, wealthier outfit bought them out. The millions Billy and his partners got for their stock financed his admission to the leisure class but did not wholly compensate him for the loss of his company. He had always believed that winning was everything, and the buy-out reconfirmed his corollary rule—that to win you had to deal from strength.

"May I express my concerns to you?" Dorothy was saying. She and the movement people she was working with had studied the numbers, "and what's overwhelming," she said, "is that there are 55,000 weapons. OK? We have about 30,000. They have anywhere from 23,000 to 28,000, depending on which estimate you believe."

A window of vulnerability had opened in her certitude, and Billy pounced. "So we really don't know what we got compared to what they got," he said.

"I think most people who are in the Pentagon will say that we are at parity," Dorothy said. *"But what is overwhelming is if you take the destructive power of all this. If you take the total air bombardment of World War II, all sides—what we dropped, England dropped, Germany, Japan—it equals about three million tons of TNT. We have in the arsenals of two countries more than six thousand World War IIs. One Poseidon submarine is equal to three World War IIs—one little Poseidon. And the new Trident—one Trident has eighty-five megatons of destructive power, equal to more than twenty-five World War IIs. And the Russians are doing the same thing. If we build three weapons a day and they build three weapons a day, when is it going to stop? When you can kill them forty times and they can kill you twenty times, what's the point?"*

"Honey, we're trying to avoid war," Billy said. "That's *the point." The ice cubes were melting into the coffee. "Now look, Dottie—it's more psychological as far as Russia is concerned. Russia is trying to spread its communistic philosophy throughout the world. Do you think they can spread that philosophy from a position of military weakness? No, ma'am! Let me tell you, honey, if I sit down to a table and I'm trying to accomplish something and those men are ten times wealthier than I am, I don't have a chance to negotiate with those people. The same thing is true with Russia."*

"You're saying we're in a psychological war—is that what you're saying?" Dorothy pressed. *"If that's true, where do you think we're going to be in the year 2000?"*

Dorothy Douglas worried a lot about the year 2000. She wondered whether there would be one. She and her teenage daughter, Laurelyn, had been watching the news one evening several years earlier and had heard Admiral Rickover, the godfather of atomic submarines, guess bleakly that there was going to be a nuclear war someday. Laurelyn, in her bathrobe, had looked at Dorothy with searching hazel eyes. She wasn't sure she wanted to grow up and have children of her own, she had said. She was too frightened of the bomb.

Dorothy's commitment to the peace movement, already begun, deepened thereafter into a fixation; until her own children figured out that she was fighting to save their future, they felt shut out of her present. She had herself come of age without thinking much about nuclear weapons, accepting on faith—her daddy's faith, really—that they were an insurance policy against war. There were duck-and-cover drills in grade school, where you curled up in a fetal position with one hand over your eyes; the teacher said not to look at the light if a bomb hit, because it might hurt you. Yellow signs went up directing people to public fallout shelters, and in the late 1950's, the neighbors dug one of their own under their garage. Dorothy watched them stock it with food and games and wondered if her parents would build one, too. Billy laughed. He had other, more pressing matters to tend to, like making money and quitting smoking. There wasn't going to be any atomic war.

The progress of the nuclear age had otherwise been part of the background noise of Dorothy's growing up, a series of bulletins that came over the TV in the den like scores in a long-running ball game. The Russians had the A-bomb. The Rosenbergs were electrocuted for telling them the secret. America discovered the H-bomb. The Russians got that, too. There were or weren't Communists in America's own government, as Senator McCarthy charged; there was or wasn't a missile gap between America and the Russians, as John F. Kennedy alleged. There were stories in the *Palm Beach Post* about something called the Red Menace. Dorothy read them and imagined human waves of Chinese coming ashore from the sea, dressed in uniform red.

But most of it was lost on her, drowned in the din of the grown-up world. Dorothy took her daddy's old yearbook from the 509th Composite Group to her Catholic high school one day, probably, she guessed years afterward, because one of the fliers looked just like Tab Hunter; the bomb then was not a matter of consuming interest to her. Her teachers were intrigued by the book. They invited Billy to speak to the students, and he agreed. He talked about his role in the summer of the bomb and the moral justifications for it—the troops assembling for a bloody invasion of Japan; the kamikaze planes sinking American ships; the necessity, in war, of taking life to save lives. He said the bomb had not outlived its usefulness, not so long as the Russians had it, too. "It is a deterrent," he said. "It is the end of all war."

"Do you really feel it was right for all those innocent ones to die?" someone asked from the back of the room. "The babies, the mothers, the children going to school?"

Dorothy could see that Billy was deeply hurt, and felt guilty for sympathizing with the question. She turned to see who had asked it. It was one of a group of visiting nuns, a small woman with tears in her eyes; her name, Dorothy found out later, was Mother Theresa.

Mostly, Dorothy inhabited the sheltered world her father had built for her. She was an all-around girl in high school, class president, prom queen, and leading lady in a school play about a gypsy princess. The color spectrum of her politics, like her daddy's, was red, white, and blue; she won awards from the American Legion and the Veterans of Foreign Wars for her patriotism. She did not trouble herself greatly with the bomb, beyond a certain limited curiosity about Billy's place in its history. The age of anxiety for her centered on whether Buddy Reynolds, better known in later years as Burt, would notice her on his visits with the girl he was seeing across the street.

Her social conscience deepened in her years at Agnes Scott College in Decatur, Georgia, studying, she thought then, to become a doctor and witnessing the flowering of the civil-rights movement. Her own upbringing had been white Southern, but the freedom spirit was catching, and she found herself, to her astonishment, arguing with Billy about the segregation and disfranchisement of the blacks; it was the first time she could remember having questioned his authority on matters of adult concern. She met Martin Luther King and Bobby Kennedy, and, from a girlfriend's house, watched Bobby's brother Jack walking on the beach out front of his family's winter compound. She was smitten with Jack and his glittery young promise; she let her schoolwork go hang while she worked for his election.

He nearly outlived her. She fell ill the year Kennedy won the presidency; she was hoarse and tired, and her hands turned purple as if she were cold. The first guess was mononucleosis. The next, and more ominous, was scleroderma, a mysterious and sometimes life-threatening malady attacking both the skin and the internal organs. Dorothy spent much of her senior year in the infirmary, getting weaker, and most of the summer afterward in the metabolic-disease unit at the National Institutes of Health in Bethesda, Maryland; it would be years before her diagnosis was downgraded to CREST syndrome, a milder form of the disease. Her roommate had been a contender for Miss America; the room was filled with the scent of roses left by her suitors, and with the expectation of her death.

The siege was an education for Dorothy, at twenty-one, in the contingency of life, one that did not end with her discharge; it could not be said for certain then whether she had two years left or fifty, and she found herself bargaining with God for more time. The illness left her with a vaguely ethereal quality, a certain porcelain thinness of feature, a slight purplish cast about the hands. But her prayer for life was granted. She spent a long introspective passage thereafter, a sorting-out period of rambling drives in the country and moments of prayer in wayside churches. The leaves had never seemed greener to her, or the sound of birds more achingly beautiful.

She was only just reentering life, studying microbiology at the University of Florida, when Moscow implanted its missiles in Cuba and the superpowers edged closer than they had ever been to the brink of nuclear war. Dorothy trusted Kennedy, but she was frightened, and she headed south in her black Volkswagen, driving closer to the missiles, to be with her parents. They waited together, and one night near the end, the three of them drove up the coast to a quiet place where Billy had often taken Dorothy fishing in her girlhood. The sky was clear and starry. They nosed their boat up the Intracoastal Waterway and out onto an inlet; then they cut the lights, dropped the anchor and fished in the still waters, with a radio playing soft music in the background. *This could be the end,* Dorothy thought. *This could be the last music I'll ever hear.* Billy was strong and reassuring. That night, the Russians backed off.

"I really hope," Billy was saying, "and I think most people hope, that we'll find some way to neutralize the atomic weapon. That's our only hope. We're not going to negotiate with the Russians. It's not to their advantage."

"Well, why not?" Dorothy asked. "They want to survive just like we do."

"Listen," Billy said. "they do not put the same price tag on life as you do or I do. You've got to understand that. Different philosophies of different people. Life to them may not be nearly as important as it is to you, basically because you enjoy life more. Your standard of living is so much higher. You weigh that against your other advantages, and they're not going to negotiate. They aren't going to give up their primary position, which they have."

"They aren't superior to us."

"Now, honey, most military men feel that they are *superior," Billy said. "You know I get the magazines. I'm telling you that the philosophy of the men who should know, and who should have the answers, is that the Russians are superior to us."*

"What difference does it make how many we have and how many they have anyway?" Dorothy asked. "I don't think we need to build any more. I think we need to look at all the other options."

"Wait a minute, now, honey," Billy said. "The Russians are trying to influence all the Latin American countries and so are we. Who influences them most—the people with the greater strength or the people with less strength?"

"How do you define strength?" Dorothy asked. "Only military?"

"No," Billy said, "I think now you can talk about economic strength if you want to. But you're already paying so much taxes now. *What are you going to do—pay more taxes so you can give those countries a better standard of living, is that what you're saying? If you are, then be willing to give up your standard of living. People are not willing to do that.* I'm *not willing to give up my standard of living."*

Dorothy produced more arguments, more numbers, and was getting nowhere. Billy had begun stealing glimpses at his watch. She had sent him some papers a couple of years before, but he hadn't read them, preferring the harder-line views of The Air Force Journal. *"No, I think we have to be strong," he was saying when she excused herself from the table for a few moments. She had been up till one that morning, reading and making phone calls, and had risen at six to start again; she was tiring and afraid her exasperation might show.*

"You have got to be in a position of strength," Billy continued in her absence. Dottie didn't understand, in

her daddy's view, having never run a company or met a payroll as he had; she had not experienced the paralysis of sitting down to do a deal, knowing all the time that the other guy had more chips. She thought geopolitics was like a marital problem, something you could sit down and talk out, when it was in fact more like business—like the time, for example, when his savings and loan was swallowed up by a bigger fish. "If you have a million dollars and I have a million dollars," he said, "neither one of us has the advantage, and you can talk about it. If you have two million and I have one million, you are going to dominate."

"Find the common denominator," Dottie said when she returned to the table.

"There is no common denominator," Billy said. "If I've got $2 and you've got $1, there is no common denominator."

The bond between father and daughter was strong, sometimes almost *too* enfolding. Billy was a tender and vulnerable man under his leathery hide and did not easily look pain in the eye; he had had a hard time visiting Dorothy in the hospital when it looked as if she might be dying, and a hard time again accepting her marriage, fearing that he might lose her. She had met John Douglas at Duke University, where she was pursuing her graduate work in neuroanatomy and he was a fellow in cardiology. They dated and, in the spring of 1967, were married. Billy was unhappy and did not hide it.

Dorothy bore a daughter and a son quickly, thirteen months apart, and, suspending her own ambitions, settled into the comfortable life of a doctor's wife. She followed John's peregrinations to teaching hospitals in San Antonio, Little Rock, New Zealand, and finally in Johnson City, Tennessee, where he became chief of cardiology at the new medical school at East Tennessee State University. Her family became her career; what energies she had left over were devoted to her avocation, weaving, and to the civic pursuits of the upper middle class: the arts council, the repertory theater, the board at the Montessori school, the League of Women Voters. She belonged to the protected world of the gentry and, entering middle age, seemed comfortable in it—a bright, attractive, spirited woman with that special quality of the heart called nurturing.

The bomb seemed a great distance from that world, impinging only at great intervals on her conscious life. In San Antonio, she had worried about the Strategic Air Command bombers flying in and out of Kelly Air Force Base, right over her head. She was sitting in her yard one day, tending her children at play in their plastic swimming pool, when one roared past at low altitude. *My God,* she thought, *that thing has nuclear weapons in it.* In New Zealand, she had watched antibomb demonstrators in boats splash a Poseidon submarine with yellow paint and, at the time, had mainly felt sorry for the sailors. But she did not engage with the subject until the night her friend Betty Bumpers called from Arkansas and asked, "Dorothy, how do you feel about nuclear war?"

The two of them had met during Dorothy's years in Little Rock, when Betty's husband, Dale, was governor of Arkansas. Their common interest then lay in programs promoting the arts, the sort of good work thought more suitable to First Ladies and to doctors' wives than worrying about the bomb. But Betty *was* worrying about it and was organizing a new group called Peace Links to educate people in the prevention of nuclear war—a women's group because women were less wedded than men to violence as a means to the resolution of conflict. Dorothy was drawn along by Betty's passion, and the night her own Laurelyn talked about not wanting to bring children into a world afflicted with the bomb, her conversion to the cause became total—so total that it crowded practically everything else out of her life.

Her first reaction was to read everything, on all sides of the subject, as if it were her doctorate she were working on and not the future of the world. She guessed later that her research had been a way to avoid *doing* anything, a last vestige of a lifetime of denial that anything was fundamentally wrong. The house was littered with her books, magazines, and learned journals, and the TV stayed tuned to cable news deep into the night; every crisis seemed to her seeded with the potential for nuclear war.

At a second stage, knowledge led to despair, at the sheer scale of the problem and at the difficulty of getting anyone in Johnson City beyond the bounds of the university campus to take her seriously. She worked the phone for hours, and even when the answers were friendly, a sense of futility sometimes came over her. *This is impossible,* she thought more than once; she was one person mixing in the business of superpower politics, a Tennessee housewife talking to other housewives about MIRVs and Tridents and the cosmic questions of war and peace.

For a passage of six months or so, her household suffered from her work and her moods. "Mom, we wish you wouldn't do this," her son, Glenn, told her once; until she made them see that she was doing it all for them, he and Laurelyn were jealous of the movement and disturbed at being asked at school if their mom was a Communist. Her marriage was tested as well. The phone bills were running to three hundred dollars a month, and the table talk had to do with the folly of mutual assured destruction, illustrated with charts of projected deaths in an exchange of nuclear weapons. John's appetite for the subject was limited, after a hard day on the cardiology service, and their life was punctuated by the sound of slamming doors. "You're *obsessed* with this!" he shouted, fleeing the house. "I can't stand it."

But he found his own way into the movement, listening to one of its spokespersons, Dr. Helen Caldicott, over the car radio one day; she seemed to be speaking to *him,* doctor to doctor, and when he got home, he asked Dorothy, "What should I do?" In three months, he had launched his own vehicle, a chapter of Physicians for Social Responsibility, and was talking throw weights and kill ratios as fluently as his wife.

Dorothy's own morale was further improved when her friend Betty took her along to a Peace Links advisory board meeting in Washington, a gathering at which everyone else was either Somebody or Somebody's wife; Betty's own husband had by then become a senator. *I'm the grass root,* Dorothy thought. Far from feeling diminished by the company, she had a sudden, empowering sense of connection with the others, a sense of shared concerns so deep that names and titles didn't matter; beneath the trappings of power and prestige, they were mainstream American women talking about whether their children were going to live or die.

She came home still high on the experience and more determined than ever to make herself heard. Johnson City remained unfertile territory, "the buckle of the Bible belt," the managing editor of the local paper called it; its politics was *arch*-arch-conservative, and Dorothy, as state coordinator for Peace Links, achieved a certain notoriety around town as "that peacenik liberal" who ran with the college crowd.

She had a rather different view of her involvement with the movement; she thought it was the most patriotic thing she had ever done. She went doggedly on with her presentations, perhaps two hundred of them, to Kiwanis and PTAs and Junior Leagues and garden clubs —anyone willing to give her and her comrades-against-arms the time of day. She carried charts and films with her, and, as audio-visual aids, a metal bucket and six-thousand BBs; she would hold the bucket up to the microphone and drop the BBs into it, one by one, making her point about the destructive force of the world's nuclear arsenal adding up to six-thousand World War IIs. The *k'chunk-k'chunk*, greatly amplified, was maddening, and was meant to be. "Stop it, that's enough!" a woman cried at one performance. That was precisely Dorothy's message.

She sustained herself with the feeling, or the wish, that the movement was growing—that it would number in the millions some not too distant day and would then be strong enough to move mountains or even governments. But her own daddy remained beyond the reach of her persuasive powers. She brought a second packet of papers to their luncheon at his club, hoping he would read them and unsurprised to hear afterward that he had not; he confessed the next time they met that he had been playing golf instead and wished she would do the same rather than worry herself to a frazzle about the bomb. She didn't have the heart to push him. He was a compassionate man, she knew that; he had even quit fishing because he couldn't stand killing fish. But she suspected that it was painful for him to look too hard at the subject of the bomb, and something protective in her held her back; she could not bear to cause her daddy pain.

"The best thing, again, Dottie," Billy was saying, "is to stay strong or to find something that will neutralize this. I think it can be done. We've gone to the moon, we have discovered laser beams, we can operate on people now without them bleeding. We have done so many things. It's not beyond our capability."

He had leapt ahead to the next generation of weapons, the proposed antimissile defense known in the headlines as Star Wars. Dorothy protested first that it would give one side an unacceptable edge in the balance of terror, and, second, that it wouldn't work. "Let's assume that we can make it 99 percent effective," she said. "If 1 percent of the weapons get through the shield, it would still obliterate the United States."

"I just told you that I feel, and a lot of people feel, that you're never going to negotiate with the Russians unless you are a whole lot stronger than they are," Billy said. He was running out of patience. "The way to get stronger, believe it or not, is to do just what you said about Star Wars. If you want to play the game, you've got to have the marbles. If you don't have the marbles, you can't play. They've got marbles and we've got marbles. No one knows who's got the most marbles."

"Say we're about equal," Dorothy said, trying again.

"Let me say this," Billy said, glancing at his watch again. "When the stakes are so high, you don't guess, because the risk is too high."

"Do you really think we can win if there's a nuclear war?"

"No, I don't believe anybody can win, Dottie honey, but there are people in the Pentagon working to prevent that from happening. I just don't think you can take the risk of believing that we are too strong."

"But can you take the risk of nuclear war?" Dorothy said.

They were getting nowhere, two people armored in certainty and restrained by love. Billy Burns was Dorothy's Rosetta stone, his resistance a code to be cracked; if she could reach him, she would have mastered the language of a generation—the generation that had brought the bomb into the world forty years ago. But she could not bring herself to press too hard, and he could not be moved. He liked her fighting spirit, the kind of attitude, he thought, that makes millionaires; he wished in hindsight that she had come into the family business. Dottie was an idealist, he thought, and he was a realist; she saw the bomb as destructive of life, where he saw it as saving lives.

Their conversation was moving in circles when they finally suspended it. Dorothy forced her papers on Billy; he dutifully carried them out to his Eldorado and waved goodbye. "Dottie, I don't want you to change my mind," he told her. His case for the defense rested on the historic fact that the planet had survived the first forty years of the atomic age. But certainty, as a condition of existence, had died at Hiroshima just after 8:15 on the morning of August 6, 1945, a casualty of the first nuclear weapon. It became the lot of humankind at that moment to live, permanently and dangerously, with the bomb.

Index